DESIGN FOR DEBAUCHERY

Also by March Hastings

Abnormal Wife
Again and Again
The Boys of Brigham Dee
By Flesh Alone
Crack-Up
The Demands of the Flesh
Design for Debauchery
Enraptured
Fear of Incest
The Heat of the Day
Her Private Hell
The Jealous and Free
Obsessed
The Outcasts
A Rage Within
Savage Surrender
The Soft Way
Three Women
The Third Sex
The Third Theme
The Unashamed
Veil of Torment
Whip of Desire

DESIGN FOR DEBAUCHERY

MARCH HASTINGS

ISBN-13: 978-1-954840-11-9

Previously published as *Fear of Incest.*

Published by
Cutting Edge Books
PO Box 8212
Calabasas, CA 91372
www.cuttingedgebooks.com

CHAPTER ONE

Eric wasn't drunk. But he was watching her and she was drunk. She was so drunk that he felt his stomach beginning to turn as she swayed around the room. All of her swayed. From the heavy breasts tumbling out of her brassiere to the stockinged feet. They looked so clean, those feet. So white and dry. She had put more care into her feet than in the feeding of her stomach. That's why she was drunk. From those whiskies on an empty stomach. He should have insisted that she eat something first. But he hadn't insisted. He never had insisted. He never even thought about insisting, as though the idea of her listening to him was more frightful than the sight of her drunk in this spring afternoon, in this golden day that opened onto New York with cool and graceful fingers. He had stayed out of work to meet her at the train, believing that their coming together again would somehow make her different.

She fell down onto the sofa, dragging her fingers unfeeling across the rattan carpet. It had been a neat, commodious apartment until she arrived. And now it was all afray, like her hair, like her wild voice ringing amuck in sentences that swung through jungles of thought and tangled them. He watched her and told himself how horrible she was, how weak and horrible he was for wanting her here, for believing she could care, could change. He felt his life sliding out of control and it made him irritable with the discomfort of losing this precious control. He thought if he got rid of her now, he would be all right forever. And he sat in his sling chair and he watched her silently and he wondered if she would have come here to him if she didn't care for him somewhere down there beneath the muddle.

"It's hot in here," she said. "Wherever I go, it's always too hot." Her voice petered out in a sigh. She stretched an arm up along the foam rubber cushion. The inside of it glistened moistly. "Open the window, Spooky. I need to feel a breeze on me."

"They're all open."

The room felt quite pleasant to him. Sounds of traffic drifted in with the slightly pungent odor from the factories along the East River. He was pleased with his apartment, satisfied that he managed his own cooking and organized a domestic routine so that he always had fresh shirts and a pressed suit. It was quite an accomplishment, after five years of married life to a woman as meticulous as his ex. But he knew that Cee-Zee wouldn't appreciate this independence that he clung to. She wouldn't understand how it felt to be the wind instead of the tide blown by it. Strength, management, building, these were phantasies she could not grasp and make real. He would have felt sorry for Cee-Zee if he could feel entirely safe from the niggling desire to impress her.

He slid out of the chair in one long motion that carried him across the room to her. He sat down gingerly beside her thighs, leaning the heel of his hand on the couch back, not wanting to touch her, not wanting to start the series of explosions inside him that could so easily shatter his good sense.

"Why don't you take a cold shower. It'll sober you up. You'll feel better."

The sunlight played on the ivory colored silk of her blouse. The soft material caressed the high swells of flesh. He wanted to put his palms one on each and press down till he felt the beating of her heart, the pulsing of blood, passionate, desirous of him. But he knew the secret of Cee-Zee and it stopped him from touching her. She was the kind of woman you didn't overbear. He had seen her turn to bored iciness beneath the insistence of a man's desire. They called her frigid, they called her teaser. And he had smiled to himself, knowing that she was certainly none of these if, *if* one were smart enough to let Cee-Zee do the chasing.

He glanced away from her to the identification bracelet on his own wrist. His name, Eric Spokane, engraved on the curve of silver looked deep and sturdy in shadow. He liked to see his name in print. On doors, on stationery, anywhere. Eric Spokane, a neat, indestructible package. Not Hilda, not Cee-Zee, not any woman could undo that package and mess it up.

"You know something?" Cee-Zee said. "You have three eyes. And they're all green." She swallowed and shut her own eyes tight. "I feel terrible." One hand groped, found his shirt cuff and pulled his fingers to her lips. She put one of them into her mouth.

He felt the sticky lipstick on his skin, the curl of her tongue around his fingernail. Quickly he reached under her back and lifted her to a sitting position, carefully removing his finger from her mouth.

"Open your eyes or you'll get dizzier."

He dragged her up onto her feet, holding her firmly around her waist. Her ribs moved rapidly in the circle of his grasp. He got her to the bathroom sink and leaned her over it.

"I can't," she gasped. "I really can't."

He turned on the cold water faucet and patted her forehead with his own wet hands.

"Leave me alone for awhile."

He judged her to see if she were steady on her feet. Her tall body, bent like a young tree, seemed strangely graceful even in this small tiled room. "Call me if you need anything." Then he stepped outside and pulled the door shut behind him.

He lit a cigarette and viewed the trickle of her belongings around the room. She had arrived without a suitcase, probably without five dollars in her purse. Of all the people Cee-Zee knew in New York, she had chosen to come to him. The thought had both troubled and flattered him all day. Now the balance was moving more in the direction of trouble. Marriage had almost convinced him that the sport of woman taming was for innocent kids. And in the first few months after his separation from Hilda, the abundance of available women had almost convinced him that the sport was even less of a sport. But Cee-Zee was fair enough game. She wasn't after his money and she wasn't after the conventional prestige of getting a Mrs. tacked onto her name. In fact, he wasn't quite sure what she wanted. But he knew what she wouldn't give up. The drifting dependence, a strange form of independence was the core of her life. She was like a war orphan who could be no further deprived. Since she had nothing, there was nothing one could take away from her. And since she wanted nothing, there was nothing one could give to her that she would value.

If he were smart, he would accept their relationship just as it stood.

He went to the kitchen and took a can of tomato juice from the refrigerator and punched two triangular holes into the top. And if he were smarter, he could get Cee-Zee to fall for him. Check-mate. And so, having defeated the worthiest opponent, he could close shop on the sport of woman taming forever. That was what he wanted, after all. To convince himself irrevocably that to be alone except in bed was the natural state of man. That this idea of love and moonbeams was nothing more than a female illusion. He poured the thick red juice into a highball glass and added pepper and salt.

The bathroom door opened slowly. He listened to the sound of her feet padding toward him. With the glass in his hand, he turned and saw her leaning sideways against the molding of the alcove. She had taken off her blouse. Wearing only her bra and skirt, she looked cooler now, calmed down. Dark streaks of water stained her blonde hair, pulled neatly back from her temples. She rubbed her nose and smiled.

"Whew." She smiled and shook her head. Her eyes seemed relaxed now. All the make-up was scrubbed off her face and high spots of color glistened in her cheeks. She seemed very young. Perhaps nineteen, perhaps twenty. Except for a small bulge of belly beneath the tight skirt, the design of her body was firm and athletic. She folded her arms and shook her head no to the tomato juice.

"Come on," he said.

"There's nothing more in me to come up."

He smiled, added gin to the mixture and drank it himself. "This is one helluva breakfast." He put the glass into the sink. "I don't suppose you'd care for scrambled eggs and toast and coffee."

She picked up his cigarette hanging on the edge of the cupboard. "I wouldn't mind."

"So long as you don't have to cook 'em."

"I wouldn't even mind that."

"Oh?"

"Well," she shrugged. "What difference does it make?"

He straddled a chair and watched her go through the procedure of arranging breakfast, noticing without surprise that she accomplished it with deftness. He wondered idly about the variety of odd jobs she must have held in the low times between lucrative boyfriends. She found the dishes and silver without asking him and set the table neatly for two with a kind of impersonal formality that gave him the feeling of being in a restaurant right in his own home. She percolated coffee and toasted the English muffins, feeling quite at ease without her blouse, adaptable to any situation, superior to most, he thought with pleasure.

They sat opposite each other and he watched her down her food with healthy appetite, her upset stomach forgotten. The steaming coffee had been properly brewed, the eggs cooked with the precise degree of fluff and dryness. He talked little and thought only of the sheer physical enjoyment of sitting before a meal which had been prepared for him. Over the second cup of coffee they lit cigarettes. Cee-Zee tilted back her head and yawned the stretching motion of contentment.

"I don't suppose you'd care to know why I came back to this stinking city in the middle of April," she said, making pictures with the matchstick among the ashes.

"I don't give a damn." His tone sounded full of conviction. He looked at the distorted reflection of himself in the chrome percolator, pleased with his nonchalance.

"Well anyway, I can stay here for a few days without getting in your way or anything? I mean, I wouldn't want to make it awkward if you have a hot affair going."

"Thanks for the kindness. But you can stay here." His manner didn't indicate that he had or didn't have involvements.

"Well, are you getting laid or aren't you?"

"I do all right."

She drew her breath in irritably. "I swear, men are the worst phonies. Look, honey, I don't care if you steal into the elephant cages at night. I'm just trying to be considerate, that's all."

"Yes, I understand." He spread his palms toward her. Her tricky temper was something he had not yet learned to anticipate. "But I'm not so involved with anyone that I'm not boss over my own apartment."

"You should have said so in the first place."

He lifted the cup to his lips so she wouldn't see the satisfaction he was trying to conceal. It was always grand to observe Cee-Zee fizzle out. Her moments of childlike helplessness were so few that it was kind of a sport in itself to accomplish.

In view of this achievement, he thought it all right to help clear the dishes. With his usual habit, he tried to stack them neatly, but Cee-Zee piled saucers on top of cups to defeat his symmetry with such effectiveness that he could hardly believe she didn't do it on purpose. She caught him beside the stove and lifted a bare elbow to his chest. "Did anyone ever tell you that you have a nasty disposition?"

"Of course. I'm famous for it."

"You are nasty and narrow-minded and probably selfish."

He kept his face rigidly serious, delighting in her intensity. "Also brutal."

"No doubt."

"Ask any of my past lovers."

"You know how I know?"

He could feel her breath on his face. Its warm moistness made him lean the slightest bit closer to her.

"By those red hairs in your sideburns. Any man who has red bristles in black hair has the vilest disposition imaginable."

"Is that why I have no friends?" He could see the pink marks on her flesh where the brassiere cut into her bosoms. He wanted to run his finger between the flesh and the material to ease the pressure.

"Poor little boy, does it need friends?"

He was at least ten years older than she, yet he did sometimes feel like a boy with her. "Yes, it needs friends."

She put her forearms on his shoulders but he did not move to grab her. He could feel it coming, the shift of her body weight against him. Still, he must not hurry her.

"If you need friends, you must learn to be friendly." Her lids had drooped slightly but he could feel that she waited alert, sensing how she stimulated herself by this foreplay.

Her arms began to move now along his shoulders till he felt the tips of her brassiere touching his chest. She began to rub them ever so slightly back and forth while she tilted her head against the side of his neck and ran the cool point of her tongue behind his earlobe. In a sudden compulsive action, she thrust herself tighty against him. His hands went down along the bare skin of her back and he gripped the solid fleshy buttocks, lifting her in one strong movement against him where it counted.

"You're such a nice boy when you behave yourself." She spoke in short breathy syllables.

"Am I behaving?" He moved himself against her in circular motion.

"Beautifully."

A dish in the sink slid over and clattered down among the silver.

"I have a lousy housekeeper," he said.

"Poor darling. Open my skirt."

He reached along to the side zipper and pulled it down. Exploring beneath the skirt, he felt the smooth half slip cling electrically to his touch. He followed the ridge of her garter belt along the contour of her thigh. He wanted to slam her to the wall and ram himself up her guts till she howled. A drop of perspiration ran down his spine and soaked into the bunched up part of his shirt tail.

"Why don't you take those silly clothes off?" she said.

"Whose?"

"Ours."

He knew he was teasing her beyond endurance and that was what he wanted. He was going to make her rape him. Then she couldn't laugh at him afterward.

The faucet began to drip with large hollow splashes.

"Let's go someplace where it's quiet," he said.

He put two fingers into the top part of her bra and tugged her gently back into the living room.

"I can still hear it dripping," he said.

"Well, I can't."

"You're just not sensitive."

He pulled her around the pine table and across into the bedroom. Bamboo blinds screened the light, throwing a gauzy pattern onto the low bed.

"You give me a hard time," she said.

"Not worth it?" He smiled, sitting her onto the bed with a sudden plop.

He fell down on his back and dragged her on top of him.

"All right," she said. "I'll undress us."

He folded his hands behind his head, watching the glisten of saliva on her lower lip. He did not relish her strangely masochistic tendency, but he respected her need.

She yanked open his belt buckle and clawed his shirt up. She flung herself face down on his belly.

"I hate hairy men," she growled.

She hated everything, she hated herself. He knew that when she ceased to hate, there'd be nothing left but a puppet of a woman.

Rocking back on her knees, she unhooked her garter belt and drew it off with her slip and skirt. She dropped her bra across his face. Its warm odor sifted into him. He lay thus with his eyes closed, feeling her hands tug down his trousers. The clink of change in the pockets came to a sudden dull stop and he knew all his clothes were on the floor. A sudden image of Hilda always insisting that he brush his teeth first and take a shower made him want to grab Cee-Zee and split her wide open with his lust.

"Come out from under there," she said.

He flung the bra aside and sat up to grasp the large brown nipples between his lips. Slowly he worked at her body, probing every curve of her, searching out the hidden places, savoring each quiver of her skin till her body lay oiled in the film of her perspiration. Staring down at her, he watched her lips twisting in wordless desire, the little veins in her eyelids blue and trembling. When he gave it to her, her nails dug into his back. He felt the throbbing of his senses and the yielding, grasping need of her body, the desire to slash her guts and ruin her for everyone else. She pulled his head down and bit his lip.

And the telephone rang with a jarring voice.

She pushed him off her and shimmied across the rumpled bed. "That'll be for me."

"You?"

"Yes, I gave this number."

"For Chrissake, to whom?"

But she was speaking into the receiver now, cuddling it to her chest.

He lay there staring at the ceiling and listening to her voice. It sounded calm and pleasant and gentle. As though she had been sitting with him in the living room all this while, drinking tea. A searing cold sensation spread slowly through his chest. He knew this sign in himself. And he knew that Cee-Zee was not going to walk out of his life until she crawled.

CHAPTER TWO

He jogged down the three flights and came out into the crush of five o'clock traffic. Giddy voices of office girls freed for a whole weekend jarred his own shell of silence. He wangled through to the curbing and proceeded along the edge of parked cars, moving steadily, rapidly cross town. It was a relief to be away from her. He strode as though to escape from the memory, as though to reaffirm his own being, his own freedom. The canvas bag with shorts and sneakers felt satisfying in his grip. That he hadn't allowed her to bug his routine felt even more satisfying. She hadn't liked the idea of going, of course. She wasn't accustomed to being anything less than the fascinating center-piece of a man's existence. Recalling her look of disbelief as he'd changed his clothes and thrown her the spare key was his only fragment of real success for the day. He congratulated himself on remembering the gym and using it to slap her face. That he would run into Hilda at the pool was certainly the lesser of the two evils, for once.

Lights recently snapped on in brownstone apartments silhouetted uniformed maids preparing dinner. He enjoyed surveying these mechanics of the comfortable East Side. A sense of solid values pervaded him. In another year or so, he too could afford this comfort. He had been successful in drawing the fine line between earning bread and earning a living. The thought made him relax a little. The quagmire of drifting was not his trap any longer. Yet he remembered the days of public johns, of hands reaching under from adjoining booths. He remembered trying to sleep in cheap movie houses and unconsciously he pulled himself up straighter as he walked, in an effort to withdraw himself physically from these thoughts. Too much of Cee-Zee in his blood and he could slip back so easily. The twelve years between then and now telescoped into a feeling of ten minutes. He recognized that Cee-Zee carried with her the flavor of his past and the recapturing of it fascinated him with a perverse attraction.

Turning off on Lexington Avenue, he went up the three steps and pushed himself through the revolving door, hurried across the lobby and down into the locker rooms. The close odor of perspiration and steam was something real, helping him to concentrate on the realities of his life as it was now. He laced the sneakers over heavy wool socks and tested the springy action of rubber soles on wooden floor. Then he went upstairs to the gym. The sight of girls flabby in their clinging black leotards grazed his consciousness. He sometimes paused to watch them working out, some with pathetic industry, others with vain attention focused on their bodies' reflection in the mirrored walls.

Now he skimmed by them, intent on his own body, the refuge of flexed muscles, the knowledge of lean good health, of a strong heart still in its prime. He stepped into the pink and chrome gymnasium. The red carpeted floor always gave him a little start of amusement. Dull, soft music seeped in to mingle with the well-oiled machines. He felt suspended in time here beneath the long fluorescent lights. For as long as he would exercise, he did not have to think about anything. The dumbbell felt cold and smooth and the room was not too crowded yet. He caught the reflection of a mustached old man straining to do sit-ups on the slant board. He saw the milk white skin of chest and arms peculiarly hairless. How many bodies there were which never saw light or air, imprisoned always in the uniforms of the wage earner. He could imagine the little wife and the three kids running the poor bastards on their treadmills to oblivion. His own skin, thank God, was still tan, if only from the quartz lamps downstairs.

At the tenth dead lift, a familiar scratchy voice said, "Hey there, Eric, what brings the boy on a Friday night?"

He finished the five remaining lifts and put down the bar. "You're looking pretty good yourself, Nat," he said, taking his towel from the bench and slinging it around his neck to mop up the perspiration.

The little wiry guy did half a dozen knee bends and yawned. "There's poker goin' on Houston Street later, if you're interested. We got some new blood."

"New green blood, you mean."

"Are you complainin'?"

"Nope." He had taken money from the table four consecutive weeks now. A peculiar run of luck that he wished would overlap into the rest of his life.

"See you there later?"

"Maybe."

Eric strolled away, not wanting to muddy his workout with talking. He couldn't seem to throw off a veil of irritation that clouded even his attitude toward poker. The small Puritron machine hummed busily, fighting to clean the air. He lay down on the slant board beside it and licked the dampness on his upper lip, unaccustomed to this restlessness that seemed to float beneath his skin. He hooked his toes beneath the leather rollers and began a rapid succession of sit-ups.

Half an hour later he had succeeded in tiring himself enough so that his thoughts lay quiet as a subdued pup. His belly felt flat and spare, neatly aligned beneath the expanse of his chest. The room had filled up now as he was leaving. He looked forward with pleasant, simple delight to lying in clouds of wet, cleansing steam.

When he reached the pool, he felt sure of himself again. Concern over Cee-Zee had somehow dissolved or stolen away to a place that he could not reach. The cold slippery tiles felt good beneath his feet and the elastic trunks hugged his flanks like tight admiring hands. He jackknifed off the spring board and glided beneath the pale, chlorinated water to surface at the shallow end. He hoisted himself up with a rush of bubbles and flipped around to sit with his ankles still in the water, shaking his wet hair back off his forehead. He sat thus for a moment gaining his breath, then stood up ready for a shallow dive.

In that instant he saw the white bathing cap, her small pointed chin held high above the water as she did her ladylike sidestroke in the shadow of the diving board.

Apparently she had seen him first because she was smiling at him while she swam. This meant she'd had time to prepare the proper expression on her features. He stood watching her move slowly toward him with her quiet, almost Oriental undulation of the body. She hardly rippled the water and her nose was still dry and powdered. She was certainly a strange fish in this water where men and women bounded around and splashed occasionally with good nature. The sight of Hilda engaged in something he knew she detested pained him. And he realized without satisfaction that she came here because it was the last thing they had ever done together. To join the gym had been her suggestion. A final attempt to build something in common. But it had failed as all her attempts had failed. It was nobody's fault, merely a simple, unfortunate lack of rapport that gave Eric a sense of being cheated which he did not want to live with. Hilda, for the sake of convention, had been willing to overlook this. Perhaps for the sake of love. But he, for the sake of life, had been unwilling to go on that way, unable to find a compromise that could rout his frustration.

He tilted his head in a polite smile of acknowledgement, knowing there was no way to avoid meeting, to avoid conversation. Automatically he walked around to the hand rails and waited there to help her up the steps.

"How nice to see you here, Eric." She stood beside him now, carefully lifting the cap away from her ears and the short dark hair. The fine texture of it curled slightly as she fluffed it out with the tips of her polished fingernails. "You haven't been here for so long, I thought you gave us up."

"I usually come on Thursdays."

He followed her to the bench against the wall, standing away from her as she patted her arms and shoulders dry. Oddly he had the sensation of not wanting to splatter her, though of course she was certainly as wet as himself.

"Well, I'm glad you decided to come tonight." She unzipped a plastic bag and took out a package of cigarettes. "I've been looking forward to seeing you. It's been so long." A note of false casualness underlined her words.

He sat down on the bench and took one of the proffered cigarettes. Her compact body seemed tense, almost shivering beneath the clinging suit. As she brought the match to her cigarette, he saw the end of it jar through the flame to touch the burning tip. This nervousness was familiar to him. He remembered the nights of her pleading in the darkness. But her sex life was none of his business any longer. He did not want to think about it nor ask if she had any friends. Yet the tight way she moved, the over-bright eyes, these revealed too plainly that she was no doubt sleeping alone. He knew the havoc a year of starvation could wreak on a constitution like Hilda's. It was a tragic irony of life that so hungry a body had been graced with the morals of a small town old maid. Eric shifted his position away from her.

"Keeping busy?" she said. "You look very well, you know. The bachelor's life must be agreeing with you."

"I'm getting along."

She laughed with a brittle sound like the shattering of glass. "You're certainly not very talkative, Eric. Such modesty implies many conquests."

He thought: Can the crap, old girl. Go out and have yourself a ball for once. Become a human being like the rest of us slobs. No one's going to feel it if you suffer except you.

Out loud he said, "I've been busy working, believe it or not."

"Oh, I believe it." She looked him full in the face. Her pupils dilated slightly in the glaring yellow light. The thick fringe of her lashes seemed to weigh down the lids as though veiling obscene, forbidden thoughts.

"And you? I suppose you've been pretty busy yourself?" He didn't want to ask, yet there was nothing else he could find to say.

"Yes, I'm fine. Very busy, as you say. To suddenly have so much freedom and no responsibilities. It's a breath of fresh air."

The lie of it gagged him. He brought one foot up onto the bench and draped his forearm on the knee, watching a fellow illustrate the Australian crawl to three young girls more interested in his blonde crew cut than in the stroke.

"I'd like to ask you over for a drink," she said. "But I do get up so early on Saturday mornings. I'm teaching French now, you know. Privately." She let the word drop with implied meaning. "Still, one must respect the schedule."

"Supposing I take a rain check on it, then."

"It's such a beautiful view of the harbor. I imagine you've forgotten that already. And only four minutes from New York."

"No, I haven't forgotten."

"If we go right away, I think it will be all right."

Before he had a chance to object, she had stood up. A voluminous smile engulfed him. "Meet you outside in fifteen minutes. I have the car."

"Hilda, I don't think..."

"Good. You shouldn't think. I know you have dozens of women waiting for you. But an hour spent with an old friend can be just as satisfying, can't it?"

Her semblance of light amusement, the effort she was making to maintain the precious pride made Eric consent. Their divorce had beaten her down so completely that he couldn't kick her again about something so meaningless as an hour or two spent in the old house.

"All right," he said. "I'll see you in the lobby."

When he came upstairs, she had not yet arrived. He went over to the candy counter and bought a magazine. No doubt, she would keep him waiting on purpose, pretending that she wasn't anxious. A year had changed her in many subtle ways, now that he thought about it. Or perhaps he was seeing her more clearly, more objectively. She seemed to be drying up, like an olive in the sun. Her slimness, her petitely youthful appearance was contradicted by the gauzy meshing of lines around her mouth. He could imagine how desperately she kept trying to buoy herself up, to maintain the gracious optimism characteristic of well-bred women. But he could see that she must be suffering from an increase of bad moments. Of doubt, of loneliness, of the fear that soon she would be old and no man would see her with the love that makes ugly oldness disappear. He wished that she could have some of Cee-Zee's nonchalance about living. And that Cee-Zee might gain some of Hilda's concern.

Hilda came upstairs ten minutes late, carrying a scarlet purse and gloves which added a touch of hopeful color to her black suit. She moved across the room with a sprightly energy that could attract many men, he thought. If only she let herself believe this.

"You look grand," he said with sincerity, as she took his arm.

"Why, thank you, sir."

They went outside and across the street to her Buick convertible. The scratches on the fender had been covered and a new black canvas top gave a smart appearance to the old car. For the first time, it occured to him that she might not be making as much money as she pretended. When she'd turned down his offer of alimony, he hadn't tried to force it on her. Perhaps now she regretted the hasty decision of her pride. But even if she were starving, he knew she would never let him know it.

She put the key into the ignition and slid over to let him drive. The familiar feel of the brake catching low toward the floor was gone. His old car, which had seen him through thousands of dusty and rugged miles across the country, was no longer the car he remembered, as the tightened brake and adjusted clutch pedal responded with a bright new reliability. And yet there were little things still the same. The corner of the glove compartment door still extended out of alignment, reminding him of the time he had pounded it with his fist because the lock had stuck. The pair of loaded dice still swung from the rear view mirror. She had not taken them off. Somehow he felt good to be driving the old jalop again. He rested back against the sagging leather and inhaled the sweet odor of gasoline.

"City driving still scares me," she murmured, crossing her legs. "I wanted you for an excuse to take me home, you know."

"Good reason." He observed that she didn't bother to tug down the hem of her skirt and it irritated him that he noticed this. The rectangular outline of her knee cap glinted from the sheen of her stocking. He tried to convince himself that she wasn't displaying her legs purposely. They were very fine legs, well molded with full calves that seemed to contradict the prudishness of her hands folded neatly on her lap. He could smell the odor of Lilac in the closeness of the car. Her subtle femininity irked him. He had no intentions of making a pass at her, she should know that. He wondered if he were driving himself into a trap by going with her.

The convergence of traffic into New Jersey moved slowly but with a steady flow. A couple of drinks, he told himself, then out. Gone, lost. Away from her. His own relaxation began to ebb and he gripped the wheel firmly, promising himself not to lose his temper with her. Funny, the way he always lost his temper with the wrong woman. Cee-Zee would appreciate a whack in the face, no doubt. But Hilda wouldn't. And yet it was always Hilda, the sweet one, the demure one who got the knocking around. He switched on the radio and let it blast too loudly.

In a few minutes she turned it down to a soft rhythm. "You seem preoccupied," she said. "I really hope I'm not taking you out of your way."

"Just one of those things," he said.

"I don't suppose it's so easy to relax in the heart of the big city. That's the lovely thing about Weehauken, I think. So far and yet so near. Always a parking space. Never too much noise."

"Look, I'm not a foreigner."

"Sorry."

He realized he was jumping at her for nothing. "Why don't you give me another cigarette?"

"Love to." She lit one for him and put it between his lips. "I've been thinking about giving up smoking," she said.

"What the heck for?" He frowned around the curling smoke.

"No reason in particular. One gets in the habit of giving up things and the habit begins to multiply all by itself. You must have given up some things in your time, Eric?" She pulled out the ash tray for him. "Remember how it felt?"

He didn't reply. She rolled down the window and put her ungloved palm up to the breeze.

"Or maybe you were always lucky enough to have something ready that could fill the emptiness."

"I don't know," he said because he had to say something. "I never thought about it."

"That's right. I forgot. You're the man who shouldn't think. Gets in your way. You're the active type, if I remember correctly. Do first then make other people think for you afterward."

He dug change out of his pocket to pay the toll. "We can spend an evening together without arguing. After all this time, we can, can't we?"

"Was I arguing, darling? I'm sorry if you thought so. I only meant to try to understand you better. And to understand myself in relation to you. I certainly don't wish to spoil our evening. After all, I'm still in love with you whether you care to hear it or not. Bold of me to say so, isn't it? Well, just take the compliment and let it pass on. There's nothing wrong with my telling you how attractive you are, is there?"

Definitely he knew now that he had made a mistake by coming with her. He could feel her desire clawing toward him from the pert little body. And he didn't want to touch her. Didn't want to become involved with her endless needing that focused on him in a burning point, magnified by the distorted thinking of her conventional mind. He threw the car into second gear to climb the steep hill to the house.

When they turned the corner and drove down the block, he felt a strange jump back into space and time. The old brick house, ten rooms of it, stood discreet, yet expectant as though it had been lying in wait for him all through the year. He felt tricked, that he had been running in circles on the end of an invisible rope which was all the while drawing him slowly in. He parked in front and sprang out, reaching instinctively into his pocket for the key to the door. A sensation of relief touched him when he realized that he didn't possess that key. He waited as Hilda took hers from her bag and turned it in the lock.

Inside the woody odor of pine walls felt good and countrified to his nostrils. She had not changed any of the furniture. The same leather chairs were in the same positions around the living room and the drawn curtains admitted the same view of the Manhattan skyline which had endeared this cliff house to him.

Without asking, she got the Johnny Walker and poured a double shot over two ice cubes and handed him the glass. He took it and went to the window to gaze out on the violet backdrop of sky. Sipping at his drink, he realized that he did not really feel he belonged in this house. Something had clicked over in his mind which closed the door against his feeling at home here. Imaginatively he stretched himself out across the river to think about his own apartment. He recollected the vision of Cee-Zee swaying drunkenly. This image stopped him from feeling at home on Second Avenue also. He seemed like an inflated balloon floating over everything, belonging nowhere.

Hilda had taken off her jacket and was sitting in the gray wing chair, her feet crossed at the ankles and propped on the matching hassock. "Beautiful, isn't it?" she said softly, sipping at her drink.

"Hm?" And he remembered that she was talking about the view. "Yes. Very beautiful."

"You know, I've never been to your new place. What is it like?" She pushed herself back on the cushion, sitting very straight, almost at right angles to herself.

"Just an apartment. Three rooms. Some chairs. A bed. What could it be like?"

"You must enjoy it."

"I do. At least I did." He turned and sat down on the windowsill. "Right now a friend of mine has taken over. I feel like an expatriate or something." He heard himself talking and wondered what was making him share these thoughts with her. The one quality about Hilda that differed from most women was that she always listened. Not with the top of her mind only, but with all of herself. She had a way of making what he said sound as though it were worth considering. This was a luxury he hadn't been able to indulge for some time.

"I hope you get your privacy back soon."

"So do I."

"You always were a softy."

"Use the right word. Sucker."

"No, I don't agree. There are limits even to your patience. I ought to know about that."

She held out her empty glass to him and he came to take it from her. He could trust Hilda not to get drunk. In all the time they had been together, he had seen her out of control only once and that was the night they had separated. A horrible experience for them both. Having seen Hilda with all her emotions showing, he understood why she never dared let herself go. A frighteningly violent person lived beneath her cool exterior. The kind of violence that did not scream and rave, but could use a knife with devastating results. Almost he could feel the small scar across his neck open again and gushing.

She got up as he took her glass and both of them went to the bar of varnished pine that he had built. "I know a lot of things now that I didn't know once upon a time," Hilda said softly.

"Let's not become analytical." He refilled his own glass.

"I don't want to analyze anything," she said. "I just want to be friends. That shouldn't be impossible, Eric. We've known each other a long time. And well." Her licorice black eyes were two wells filled to brimming with intimacies shared between them. "I don't see that there's anything wrong with two people being ... friends." Her gaze seemed to reach out to him. She tried to smile. But her look was beseeching. She drew a quick little breath. "I'm not as busy as you are. Not really. Oh, there are things and people. But I don't seem to have your knack for getting close."

He turned away from her and put his hands flat down on the bar top. It's surface felt slick and cold.

"I don't seem to have any knack at all." Her voice reached round him, warm and suffering.

"Hilda, let's be honest with each other." He spoke without turning. Not wanting to see the imploring in her eyes, he spoke toward the walls. The photographs he had taken on their cross-country trips seemed dark and haunted in the fading twilight. "We couldn't make it then. There's no reason to think we can now. I'm very fond of you and I respect what you are." He shook his head slowly. "But we don't meet anyplace. We just don't meet."

He felt her hand on his back. His skin prickled in the area of her touch. "I was selfish," she said breathily. "I've learned not to be selfish anymore. It's no fun being alone, darling. I lie in the huge bed every night." Her voice choked off.

"You're a young and beautiful woman. If you'd give yourself the chance to accept people . . ."

Her hand began to move downward along his spine. "I want to give myself that chance. I want to accept you. As you are. I don't want to change you and try to make you conform to silly rules of behavior that don't make any difference. Can't you understand me, Eric? You were the first man in my life. There can never be another one who means as much to me. When I think of love, when I think of belonging, I think of you. Only you." Her arm slid around his waist. She opened the button of his shirt and he felt the edge of her nails gently against his belly.

He pulled away from her. "I'm sorry, Hilda." Now he turned to speak straight into her begging, upturned face. "I believe you and I appreciate your loyalty. But I can't."

"You never really did find me attractive, did you, Eric?" Her voice was a trifle shrill. "You didn't go for virgins. They bored you. And I'm still a virgin because no other man has touched me. So I still bore you." A pale blue vein stood out on her forehead. "I know how it is with my Eric. He needs violence and profanity. He needs sluts who spit on him afterward. He needs to pay for abortions he isn't even sure are his own." She whirled and strode off to the window, flinging it up and breathing deeply as though all the air had been cut off from her. "Sometimes I wonder why you aren't dead of some filthy disease." She rapped her knuckles in anguish against the window frame. The wind lifted her hair in little whisps and wafted her perfume back toward his nostrils.

"Good-bye, Hilda. I'm sorry." Buttoning his shirt, he started toward the door.

"No, don't!"

Her heels clicked rapidly on the floor and she stood blocking his exit, her thin arms extended.

"I didn't come here to fight with you. Let's cut this thing clean," he said. "It's no use. You see that."

"Let's make believe," she said desperately. "We never met before. We don't know anything about each other. Two strangers. I asked you in for a drink." She took his hand and tried to pull him back to the bar. Her skin felt clammy. With trembling movements, she poured his glass full. "There. Now I'll say, Mr. Spokane, you sound like you're in a very interesting business. Tell me about life insurance. I've been thinking about taking out a policy, only I don't know which one would be best for me."

He felt all curdled inside. "I don't want to drag this out, Hilda. Please let me go."

"Why, Mr. Spokane, don't you enjoy selling insurance? Doesn't it fascinate you, all those millions of dollars that pass through your hands every month?"

Her mouth was slightly open and she spoke as though her tongue were thick and dry.

"Hilda, I want to go."

"Well then, we can talk about photography, shall we? I'm thinking of buying a Rolliflex. Would you advise it?"

"Hilda."

"You're not giving me a chance. You're not. You're not! Do I have to throw myself at your feet and bleed? Do I have to lower myself beyond humiliation?" She reached out and clutched the collar of his jacket. "Stay with me just this once, Eric. I'm begging you, can't you see that?" Her voice splintered away into silence. She rested her cheek against him now. Her arms hung helplessly at her sides as her body shook with sobs that she could not control.

He put his hand on her hair and began to stroke it. The knowledge of Hilda's body forcing her to do this thing, so shameful in her own eyes, made him gentle. Sometimes in the past, he had wondered if there were any woman so cursed as Hilda by cravings she couldn't bear to face. Yes, he could stay with her this one night, but what would it solve? She would need it again and again. Her nature demanded it. She could not direct her energies sufficiently into other channels. Heaven alone knew how hard she must have tried. But he must not make the mistake of getting involved with her again. He did not want to be a stud horse for her.

"I need you," she sobbed into his jacket. "God help me, but I need you."

In a sudden flash of anger, he wondered what kind of catastrophe would make Cee-Zee say these words to him. He closed his eyes for a moment and Hilda became the tanned careless creature who had drifted into his world. He put his lips down to her head and held her close.

"Honey, it's all right," he whispered. And the Lilac perfume became the soapy smell of Cee-Zee.

He pulled himself out of it with a jolt but Hilda was already in his arms, her lips reaching eagerly up toward his own.

I must be nuts, he thought.

But he began to kiss her. His body stiffened, wanting to thrust her from him.

"I knew you would be good to me, darling," she whispered against his neck.

The words made him feel nauseous and stupid. Something was all twisted, all wrong. He had no business letting himself get so out of hand about Cee-Zee. He certainly had no business allowing this with Hilda.

Phoney, selfish bastard, he thought. And weak. God damn it, weak. Where were his rules, where were his guts? He wanted to kick his own teeth in and get on a tramp steamer and disappear someplace into Asia.

"You're the one thing that can protect me from myself," Hilda whispered.

Yeah, sure, he thought, and wondered how one woman could be so far off.

"Kiss me, darling, just a little."

What the hell, he thought. The world goes round anyway. Cockeyed round. Daisy chain round. *Peter loves Mary who's hot for a fairy…*

"Eric, hold me tight. Squeeze me."

The wind rustled a magazine on the table. He put his arms around her fragile body. He could break her in half without trying. The muscles of his forearms flexed, pressing into her back. He heard the breath go out of her.

He bore down on her open mouth and felt her lip go back hard against her teeth. A sound grunted deep in her throat. She struggled but he held onto her, bending her head back on her neck almost hoping it would snap off. Lifting her from the floor, he lay her down on the hassock so that it supported the small of her back.

"On the couch, darling," she muttered. "More comfortable."

"Shut up."

She twisted away and rolled onto the floor. He grabbed for her. The material of her blouse shredded in his hands.

"Eric, you're wild," she rasped.

"You wanted it, bitch."

He dragged her to him and flung all of his weight on her small frame. Without care, he yanked at the skirt and her underthings till she lay naked and bruised on the hard cold wood. Her compact breasts quivered, her stomach heaved. She spread her legs. Her eyes seemed to roll up dizzily. "You need me, you need me," she grunted.

He could have killed her. "I don't need you for anything." The words were hardly audible.

"You need me."

Sparks of electricity seemed to be shooting out from him in the echo of this lie. He knew it was so. He didn't need her, not for anything. But it was she who needed him, craved him, and was lying there sick with this craving. A surge of power filled him. His insides felt phosphorescent with the strength of command over her. For a moment, he held himself away.

"Eric. Take me."

"I'll take you. In my own good time."

The cruelty broke through his dam of reserve. He held himself away as she arched her body toward him, her white skin taut and rippling with eagerness. Her hand groped blindly till it found his neck. She tried to drag him down to her but he held himself away, running his hands all over her body, biting these same paths of flesh and feeling her quivers of pain and delight blending into each other and chasing her high to the peak of desire.

Her hips began to move in an arching circular motion. The speed increased as though she were mentally obtaining what he withheld from her.

"Damn you, Eric. I want it now!"

"Savor it, baby. Give yourself a chance to appreciate."

"You're driving me crazy."

"We're all crazy," he muttered to himself.

The shadows of night covered their nakedness and they lay as though in the Garden of Evil.

He felt her body shudder and heave as he moved into her. Her voice tore on a long intake of breath and she laced her arms and legs around him. Rhythmically and hard, he heard her buttocks slapping with dull thuds on the unyielding floor. Her body raced on faster and faster. Then with a little cry, she became rigid, her back poised in mid air. Slowly her bruised thighs relaxed away from him.

Sometime, it felt like hours later, she rolled away and lay beside the legs of the couch. He had gotten up and was standing, still naked, at the bar, drinking alone.

"You think I'm a tramp, don't you?"

The words were too profoundly ridiculous. He didn't bother to answer.

"I said, you think I'm a tramp, don't you?"

"I don't think anything. I'm in no position to judge anybody. Least of all you."

She sat up slowly and rubbed her hips. “I’d be better off dead, wouldn’t I?”

He finished the Scotch in two large gulps, feeling it burn down his gullet. But it could not burn away the isolation that smothered him. “Stop torturing yourself,” he said. “You’re making a big thing out of nothing.”

“I’d be better off dead if I didn’t know that I could count on seeing you again.” Her words were dull with conviction.

He saw her breasts outlined in the window.

“Close it,” he said. “It’s getting chilly in here.”

“I don’t know why it has to be you I love,” she said, pulling the window down slowly. “But nobody else could do what you’ve just done for me.”

“Have you tried?” he answered matter-of-factly.

“There are some things a woman knows instinctively.”

“Rot.”

“I don’t expect you to believe me.”

He moved in the darkness to find his clothes and pulled them on slowly. All of him ached as though he had stood up for a month. A slight throb was beginning in his temples and something seemed to be pushing from the insides of his eyeballs. He got himself dressed, jamming his tie into the pocket of his jacket.

“Are you going to leave me, just like this, in the middle of nowhere?” she said.

“Believe it, baby, you’re not alone.” His words came out with unexpected bitterness.

“Do something for me,” she said, coming close to him.

“Sure, if I can.”

Her hand moved among the glasses and bottles on the bar and he heard her rings clink against them. Then he felt her hand drop something into his shirt pocket. He reached up to find the outline of a key in it.

“Whenever you want to,” she said. “I’m not the kind to play hard to get.”

He swallowed, thinking he would drop the damn thing into the sewer when he got outside. "But I don't want you to sit here waiting for me."

"What else have I got to do?"

"Teach French."

He didn't wait for further conversation, but got the hell out of there, knowing that Hilda at least would have a good night's sleep.

CHAPTER THREE

For a few blocks, he walked quickly along the drive. It was past ten o'clock and the streets were quiet. The emptiness and the calm slowed him. He stopped to gaze at the midtown lights shimmering on the black water. The pungent odor of tar and moss from the boat pilings drifted up to him and he thought how good it would be to ride back on the ferry. But then he turned and headed for the bus stop because he was beginning to recall the times he used to ride that ferry with his brother during the hot summer months. Years ago, when he was a kid. Girls were nothing to him then, compared with hand ball or shooting craps against the garbage cans.

The bus was empty too, except for an old woman carrying flowers wrapped in a newspaper. He sat down on a rear seat and let himself jounce along with the loose springs. His mind kept returning to the image of Hilda, small and incompetent in her sprawling house. He remembered the key in his pocket and smiled, knowing he wouldn't throw it away after all.

He stepped out into the congestion of New York, more comfortable, more anonymous here. A line of taxis parked in front of the bus stop. He got into the first one, directing the cabbie to Houston Street. Something uneasy in him didn't want to go home yet. He stretched his feet to rest them on the folded jump seat, whistling a silent accompaniment to the dissonance of his nerves.

The cab stopped and let him out in front of a closed bakery. On the corner people gathered in front of a large delicatessen but the middle of the block was dark. He went in through a small door next to the bakery and started to climb the narrow, musty stairs. The dank wood yielded tiredly beneath his weight. He took the steps three at a time till he reached the top floor. He joggled the loose knob and Nat let him in.

"Man, we've got plenty of action tonight." He winked and motioned Eric to the table with a stabbing action of his chin.

The room was a large bare place with dark green curtains hanging at the windows. A round slate table stood in the center where five men were watching the dealer shuffle. Cigar and cigarette smoke hung in wavy disks beneath the ceiling light. Three of the men nodded hello as Nat brought a chair up for Eric.

"The one behind the bills is Joe Conaty," Nat said with good nature.

Eric saw a stack of twentys and tens anchored by a cigarette lighter.

"Sit down," Conaty said. "You can help me keep this growing."

"Sure," Eric said. He had thirty dollars in fives and singles. He took the fives out.

"That won't help much," Conaty said, running a palm over his bald head. A line of freckles indicated where his hair had grown.

"Let's play," one of the other guys grunted.

They were all good boys. Shrewd players, Eric knew. The Friday night game was ritual with them. Where they scattered to during the week, how they scrounged up enough for the two and five ante, he didn't know and cared less. Eric adjusted himself on the straight backed chair and watched the dealer's smooth fingers parcel out for five card draw.

Eric fanned his cards to see a pair of treys. He sat one removed to the left of Conaty which meant he could take his cue from the new man's betting. Conaty opened.

"Call."

"Call."

Everybody stayed.

"I'll take two," Conaty said.

"Three for me."

"Two dollars," Eric said. He lifted his cards one at a time to find that he hadn't improved his hand. The treys and jack high.

Conaty said, "I'm in for five."

"Drop," said the man between Conaty and Eric.

Eric smiled inwardly, sensing Conaty's eyes on him. He didn't glance back, but put his five into the pot.

Everyone else dropped except Nat. Eric knew from experience that Nat stayed only when he had a powerhouse. But apparently his cautious playing wasn't doing so well tonight. Eric saw Nat's cards curved in the palm of his hand. It could mean that he was bluffing. He might have lost too much already this evening. He could be sticking out of sheer nervousness.

"No raisers?" Conaty smiled. His gray eyebrows twitched with satisfaction.

Conaty put an ace on the table.

Eric spread his pair of threes.

They both turned to Nat and saw him drop his cards, face down.

The game went on, Eric slowly boring a hole in Conaty's bills. He kept taking small pots but the money was obviously shifting toward him. He felt that he was getting on Conaty's nerves. To win consistently with small cards was like hitting a man below the belt. But he had been riding this streak for over a month now and Eric felt that it was never going to break. All his coordination, all his force seemed to focus in his gambling. It had been like this when he was in the Army. He had stopped playing when he had married Hilda. She hadn't thought it quite respectable. Truly, he didn't care whether he played or not. But he did want the choice to make his own decisions. His old self, moving fast and alone, was a satisfying feeling and he enjoyed the game now because of the wild times it brought back to him.

He cut out of the game at two thirty.

"I'll see you next week," Conaty said.

"Right."

He folded the hundred and fifty and went outside. The depressed feeling had left him. The throbbing in his temples was gone and his body felt alive despite the sitting for all those hours. He stretched in the cold night air, hiked up his trousers and grinned at the sliver of moon riding high behind a haze of clouds. He strolled twenty blocks up First Avenue and took a bus the rest of the way home.

It was past three when he put the key in the lock.

The apartment he entered made him stop short at the door. Paper cups spilled amongst ash trays piled high in dishes with bits of food on them. Potato chips were rubbed into the carpet. The place stank of liquor.

Cee-Zee sat cross-legged on the floor beside his radio, its guts spread around her. A little ball of a man puffed the stubby end of a cigar, hovering over Cee-Zee with a screw driver in one hand and a roll of bicycle tape in the other.

"Hey, Spooky," Cee-Zee said, "you keep any spare tubes around this place?"

He picked his way through the litter and glared down at the plethora of screws and nuts. "What the hell are you doing to that poor radio?"

"What does it look like I'm doing?"

"Butchering it."

She shrugged and pulled herself to her feet, hoisting herself up by the fat man's trousers.

"You missed the party Lilio gave for me."

"And who the deuce is Lilio?"

"That is I." The fat man put down the tools and tugged the points of his striped vest. He had managed to combine a gray striped suit with a gray striped tie so that Eric's eyes were led up the front of him to land on his fleshy red nose pitted with thousands of blackheads.

"Oh, don't you know Lilio?" Cee-Zee sounded genuinely surprised. She leaned over and put her arm around his gross middle. "I thought everyone in the world, at least in New York knew you. Aren't you famous?"

Lilio chuckled with a self-deprecating quiver of his narrow slanting shoulders. "Sometimes it misses a few people."

"If you both don't mind, I'm going to sleep," Eric said. "And I'll expect this mess cleared away by the time I get up, Cee-Zee. Famous Lilio can help you if he isn't too famous." He turned and stalked into his bedroom, slamming the door to shut out the mess and confusion. He took off his clothes and climbed into bed, determined not to think about it. If he thought three consecutive sentences, he knew he'd go outside and wallop somebody. He climbed in beneath the sheets and pulled the covers over his head, shutting his eyes tight and training his mind on the vision of four aces.

The sound of their voices drifted in through the door, through the blankets. He felt his legs stiffen. He put the pillow over his head. Their voices came through the pillow too. He sat up. He jumped out of bed and strode to the door in his jockey shorts. He pulled the door open to see Lilio adjusting a navy homburg on his slicked head.

"I am just now leaving so you can sleep well, monsieur."

Cee-Zee looked him up and down. "Spooky, you're just too much tonight."

"I am leaving now. Au revoir. So sorry you do not appreciate a little bit fun sometimes."

He was out the door before Eric could answer him.

"Well now, isn't this nice of you?" She sauntered up to him with one hand on her hip. "I might have known you're too Goddamned narrow minded or stupid or something. Or maybe it's because you're poor, I don't know. So he isn't beautiful and we wrecked your precious nest a little bit. It wouldn't occur to you that I've got my reasons. No. All you can see is your own selfish, possessive... Oh, I can't even talk to you." She whirled around and plumped down onto the couch. "If I'm such a pain, maybe I'd better leave."

"So leave!"

He turned to go back to bed but this time he didn't close the door. After awhile he heard her get up and begin to collect the debris.

The dull pink of dawn had started to lighten the sky. He lay on his belly wide awake, the covers pushed to one side. Occasionally he heard her sigh or turn the page of a book or get herself a glass of water. She hadn't gone to sleep. Like some strange amphibian crawling between light and dark, she didn't seem to need rest. He wondered about the twisted forces driving her to scatter her life so uselessly. And he told himself he didn't care. Not about her and not about her reasons for encouraging a friendship with the likes of that pig Lilio. No doubt the man had money. He'd probably offered to keep Cee-Zee. On her own terms. It was odd that she hadn't accepted him yet. It wouldn't be the first time.

Stonily he waited, convincing himself that Cee-Zee would come in and apologize. He was determined not to make the first move toward her. If he did, he could see where the path led. His costliest possession was not his home but his independence. She wouldn't know about such things.

Fingers of pain poked into the back of his neck and his tongue felt large and swollen in his mouth. He wished he could fall asleep but his mind remained stubbornly alert. He realized that he was actually expecting her to come in and he laughed at himself for thinking like a jerk.

The alarm clock went off in the middle of nowhere. He reached out a hand and pushed the stem in.

"You work on Saturday?" she called in.

He knew this was her excuse to start conversation. "No. I forgot to turn it off yesterday."

"How do you feel?"

"Lousy. Why?"

"I don't know. I feel lousy too."

"You should," he said flatly.

"Well, I'll be out of here soon and you can get some sleep."

Her words were testing him. He felt too tired to play games. "You know damned well you aren't going anywhere."

Cee-Zee came to stand at the door. She stroked an earlobe as though it were worn out from too much jewelry. "I don't know any such thing. After all, I counted on you for something and look what happened to me."

He sat up and pulled the covers around his waist. The ring of her voice sounded sincere. It put him off guard with curiosity. "What did you count on me for? Come here and tell me."

She remained standing in the doorway. "I know what'll happen if I come over to that bed."

"You couldn't be more wrong." He had to smile. The hours with Hilda had drawn more of his energies than Cee-Zee could suspect. He would be up to it if she made herself more enticing. But he was sure as hell he wasn't going to run after her. He folded his arms. "O.K. Stand there as long as you want, but go on talking."

Her hair fell in straggles over the ears, giving her a jungle look. The skin pulled tautly across her high cheek bones and her wide lips jutted with petulance. The sad child in her was seeping through. Eric knew that this was her most dangerous self. Her knack for softening a man up. It worked because she herself believed in it for a moment. The only difference was that this sadness could dissolve, also childlike, in an instant. And he'd be caught off balance.

"You said you counted on me?" he repeated carefully.

"Well, yes. But it's embarrassing to talk about. After all, I wanted to impress Lilio. He shouldn't think I needed him for anything. You know what those characters are like. One whiff that a girl is interested and they take advantage. Clam up. Become stingy. They certainly don't propose marriage."

A shock ran through him. "Am I hearing you right?"

She came over now and sat down on the edge of the bed. From her brassiere she took out a wad of bills. "Does it really surprise you that much? Do you think that people like me don't get tired of living out of suitcases?" She fanned the five twenties out on the mattress. "You know what I did when he gave these to me the first time? I threw them back in his face. He had to force 'em on me. At least that's what I made him think." She laughed acidly. "I told him I had a good thing in you and didn't need his money. And just because I said that, he's going to come back. He'll think he's fighting for me. At least I hope he will, after that performance you put on."

She let herself fall backward onto the bed across his legs.

"I think we should have a cigarette," he said. "There's something here you're not figuring right."

"It's figured right," she said. "You just can't believe it. Settle down and it'll make very good sense even to you."

He gazed unseeingly at the movement of her diaphragm and tried to get his bearings parallel with the way she was thinking. No matter how he looked at it, the prospect of Cee-Zee sleeping with that repulsive creep was fantastic. Sure, he could see her marrying someone for money. But she was still young and plenty appealing. There were lots of men with money who didn't look like Lilio.

"Is it just his money you're after?"

"He's good to me. And he'll keep being good because I know how to work on him."

"What do you mean by good to you?"

"Freedom."

"Don't kid yourself."

He shifted over to the night table and fished out a cigarette from a half emptied pack. Struggling to be analytical about this crazy scheme, he knew he wasn't really thinking straight at all. A flush of irritation clouded his brain. Quite possibly, she could pull this thing off. She might even manage her so-called freedom once she had the wedding ring. But it was all wrong, even if he couldn't find the gimmick. An uncomfortable sensation of being used pervaded him. Yet she was honest. And if he had let her speak, she'd have told him about this yesterday.

"Look, Spooky, you know me as well as anyone. I have no stability. No security. I can't go on like this. It's too much of a mishmash. Sure it would be fine if I could fall in love with somebody. But there isn't that somebody around who's stronger than I am."

Her words cut him right through the middle. "Maybe you haven't been looking."

"Now don't *you* kid yourself," she said. She put out her hand and took his cigarette.

It irked him that she could be so blind. Once again she had unwittingly rammed home the fact that he meant nothing to her. Friendship didn't seem to count for much.

"All right," he said after awhile. "If you think Lilio is what you need, I'll back you up." He mashed out the cigarette butt and straightened the covers. "Now let's see if we can get a little shut-eye."

He waited until she had taken off her clothes and crawled in beside him. Then he closed his eyes and let his mind wander. The sport of Cee-Zee was beginning to take on unexpected complications. But there was one encouraging aspect. She was beginning to depend on him for help. He could encourage this dependence, until eventually she would be forced to see that neither love nor money were the really powerful forces in her life.

The thought relaxed him and he drifted off to sleep.

He awoke late in the afternoon to feel her breathing against him. She was still fast asleep, her legs intertwined with his, her cheek nuzzled to the side of his chest. A faint dampness glistened on her forehead. In repose she looked sweet, unlined, innocent. He shuddered to think what dreams were reeling off behind that innocent face. She sighed gently and snuggled up closer, her warm breasts flattening out against his side.

There were other things to do besides think about Cee-Zee, he told himself as he turned and tried to move an arm out from under her head. Prospects to see for dinner. Prospects meant commissions. And commissions meant a promotion. He had a pad full of telephone numbers which he'd meant to call yesterday. Now they'd have to wait for Monday morning. He remembered his date tonight at Martin Millardson's. To snag the Millardson account would be quite a boost. He twisted around to look at the clock. Two hours to get ready.

He worked his way out of the bed, managing not to waken Cee-Zee and headed for the shower. The buzz of his electric shaver made a loud noise and he heard Cee-Zee turn over in bed.

"Spooky?" Her voice was rusty with sleep, but anxious.

He moved the door open with his foot. "I'm in here."

"What's happening?"

"Nothing. I'm just getting cleaned up."

"Oh." She pulled the covers back over her head and he closed the door again.

The needle shower felt hot and good across his shoulders, working the knots out. He stood in the spray letting it pound him and wishing he could get it even hotter. As he worked the lather down his legs, the door opened. Cee-Zee came in, shutting the door behind her.

"I'm using your toothbrush."

"Enjoy yourself." He was busy scrubbing arms and legs, thinking how best to work on Millardson this evening. They had met twice before. Eric knew that Millardson had a sense of humor and plenty of kids who knew how to spend his money for him. Millardson spoke about them affectionately and Eric got the idea he was a contented sort, proud to have come up the hard way and complacent about having it to squander on his family.

"You're taking all day," Cee-Zee called.

"Then you can take all night," he answered.

She pushed aside the shower curtain. The water splashed on her face and she squinted. "Oh, no. I'm coming in right now." She stepped over the ledge, hunching her shoulders in the quick rush of water and rubbed herself against Eric. "Let me under, hog."

He turned her around and began rubbing the soapy cloth across her back, feeling her sigh and relax. Then he reached with the soap down the front of her, moving the bar beneath her breasts and in circles along the lower part of her belly. She took his hand with the soap and guided it to make a triangle of bubbles. "Mmm. Nice," she gurgled, holding her head away from the spray.

She slipped around in his arms and took the soap from him, rubbing it vigorously at his chest. Then she dropped it to the floor and backed him up against the wall of the shower booth.

"Hey," he said. "Take it easy. I don't have time."

"Time? What the hell is that?" She grinned at him through the drops of water running down her cheeks. She looked very kittenish, very rested, her troubles of the previous night already forgotten.

Eric put his hands on her hips and moved her away from him, laughing because it was pleasant to fool around like this, almost wishing he did have another hour or so for her. "Come on now, quit it. I've got an appointment tonight. You're going to make me late." He tried to get around her to step out of the shower.

"Phooey to you and your appointments." She hooked her arms around his neck with purposefulness, her soapy smooth breasts sliding around on him.

He knew it was no use arguing. He couldn't expect her to honor his responsibilities. With a powerful determined gesture, he reached behind her and turned on the cold water full force.

With a screech, she bounded away from him and out onto the bath mat. He turned off the faucets and stepped out beside her. She stood shivering, her mouth drooping a little with annoyance. "You're pretty high falutin' today, mister."

"I told you. I've got an appointment." He lifted a turkish towel off the hamper and began rubbing himself briskly. "Business. You know what that is, don't you?"

"I'll bet." She took an end of the towel and began patting her chest.

"Seriously, I have this heavy prospect on the list tonight. The kind of thing that brings in green stuff. Money. Remember money?"

"Oh yes, I remember money all right."

But she didn't remain subdued for very long. She pulled the towel away from him altogether and let it drop between them. "Take me with? If it's only business, I'm a very fine asset to have around." She waggled a finger under his nose. "I have a way of softening the enemy."

He stepped over to the sink, wiped the vapor from the mirror on the medicine cabinet and took a comb out, running it quickly through his wet hair. "Not this enemy, sweetie pie. This is a married enemy. A happily married enemy."

"No such thing." She picked up the towel and drew it between her thighs.

He didn't bother to answer her, knowing she could not concede the possibility of a working marriage. And she was so far off the beam about Martin Millardson of all people that it was ridiculous to talk about him.

"I didn't hear you objecting," she said.

"Let's drop the subject."

"Because I'm right?"

"Because you're so very wrong." He handed her the comb and went out into the bedroom.

She came after him, the towel hanging between her legs. "Okay, I don't want to be a drag."

"Good girl." He pulled on fresh black socks and got his black shoes from the closet. Because she had given in so amiably, he felt suspicious.

As he continued to dress, she spread the towel on a chair and sat down, draping her legs over the arm rest and leaning back to enjoy the wash of cool air over her nakedness. "I guess I'll just rest up while you're gone. How late will you be?"

"Not too. Maybe eleven, twelve."

"You have to be tactful about these things? Friendly like, huh?"

"Sure."

"What a bore." She sighed and closed her eyes, slowly lifting her damp hair away from her neck and letting it fall.

Silently, he agreed with her. He didn't much care for the hail-fellow-well-met necessary in his job. The art of public relations was something he had a knack for but he wasn't proud to use it. But it was part of the game. He had wrestled this point with himself months ago and decided that a little lip was worth the pay involved. He took a pair of onyx cuff links from the drawer and slipped them through the French cuffs of his shirt. Then he got the dinner jacket and trousers and hung them on the edge of the closet door so he could brush the few bits of lint from the shoulders.

"Pretty snazzy affair," Cee-Zee commented.

"Just part of the routine."

"Well, I hope it's worth all the effort."

"So do I."

She began to hum a little song to herself, spreading her tanned limbs and swinging them casually. "You said about eleven?"'

"Um hm." He was busy transferring all the necessary papers to the inside pocket and checking the contents of his pass case and the bills in his wallet. The hundred and fifty made a comfortable bulge in the morocco leather. He had to admit to himself that it was nicer earning a living at the card table than the dinner table. But he wasn't supposed to think that way anymore. Drifting, idling had gotten him pretty low, once. The conveniences of being a solvent citizen were worth all the inconveniences. He slapped the dresser drawer shut and saw that it caught on the strap of his camera case.

Pushing the camera further back into the drawer recalled Hilda and the early days of their marriage. He smiled sourly at her words of faith to him. They'd proved so hollow. Often he had tried to understand why Hilda had wanted to fool herself into believing she could be happy living on the sporadic income of a free-lance. The first year, her brave attempts were almost successful. She'd even learned to develop negatives to save part of the expense. Doggedly he tried to think that she was content travelling around the country, going to weird places at all hours of the day and night for the sake of special shots. And then the headaches, the tiredness, the inertia began. It wasn't long before the diagnosis of her trouble was plainly evident. So he gave in and opened a photo supply shop. But he couldn't make out with this compromise. Finally, in a flash of good sense, he got rid of the store, got rid of Hilda and went into insurance to pay off the debts.

He knotted the black bow tie and pulled the wings tight, surveying his appearance, his nostrils picking up the odor of after-shave lotion still brisk on his chin. Mentally checking his belongings, he was all set.

"See you." He bent over and kissed her a friendly peck on the forehead.

Her fingers squeezed him on the inside of his thigh. "Have a wonderful business," she said.

"Check."

He went out and hailed a cab to the Fifth Avenue residence, trying to shake off the uncomfortable suspicions about Cee-Zee that still pervaded him.

CHAPTER FOUR

He strode under the long electric blue canopy past three doormen in blue and gold uniforms into the glassy plush entrance foyer and pressed the elevator button. Potted elephant ear grew on either side of the lift, its heavy gloss-green leaves bending down to the circle of earth. He dropped his cigarette butt into the damp soil, figuring how many times a day one of the doormen had to come pick them out, cursing slobs like himself for messing up the expensive decor.

The ride up to Millardson's penthouse was rapid and effortless, the square polished cage jumping eagerly like another anxious, underpaid servant. He touched the doorbell and heard the bing-bong echo softly inside. He waited, conjecturing about how far he was willing to put himself out for the Millardson account.

A maid in starched black nylon with a white starched apron over it opened the door to him, her servant's smile coldly warm but dimpled and charming nevertheless. She said, "Good evening, sir," with a rolled r sound. He hoped she would learn another trade in this country. Make better use of her rosy complexion and healthy peasant body.

Because it was warm, he had forgotten to wear a hat and she had to stop herself from asking for it as he came inside. He winked at her and grinned, noting her finely chiseled ankle bones and finding it a crime that her lovely legs had to be undermined by the lace-up, heavy heeled oxfords.

"I'm Eric Spokane," he said kindly and wanted to add: what's your name and when do you get out of this dump?

"I'll tell Mr. Millardson you're here."

"Thank you."

He watched her almost bow herself out, making him feel like some kind of phoney royalty. When and if he got this kind of money to throw around, he'd dress his girls in leopard skin suits or maybe pink nighties.

He came further into the room, surveying the gold antique mirrors and brocaded Louis XIV chairs, marvelling at the lack of imagination someone had used in furnishing. The place reminded him of a typical movie set and he could see the old lady of the house corseted breathlessly into her champagne colored dress. He sighed, picturing Cee-Zee at home romping around in her skin. The starched collar cut stiffly into his neck.

"Eric old man, glad you could make it."

"Good evening, Mr. Millardson." He grasped the extended hand of the well-knit little man bouncing toward him and smiling broadly behind the thick glasses. The frames emphasized a young shrewdness that seemed to contradict the leathery rolls of age bunching his neck. The sagging skin looked more like a bag pulled over his head with two holes cut in it for eyes rather than part of himself.

"You'd better call me Martin," he said, "or my kids'll laugh at you for being a pompous old goat. What're you drinking?"

"Scotch and water'll be fine, Martin."

Their shoes clicked like race plates on the black and white marble floor as they moved through the hallway into a room lined up to the ceiling with books. A pool table stood in the middle of the carpet with two cues crossed on it.

"I don't know who's coming for dinner," Martin said. "Anybody's liable to fall in. I hope you're prepared."

"Always prepared," Eric said, taking the glass and sipping from it.

"Good boy. We'll see if we can stir up a little trouble for you. Never met my kids?"

"Never had the pleasure." He thought it curious that Millardson always spoke about his children and never mentioned his wife.

Millardson jumped up on the edge of the pool table and swung his legs. "How about you? No family started yet? Smart thing to get in on the ground floor. I don't go for these bachelors prowling around town. Pub crawling idiots. 'Bout time you became a family man."

"Well, I try."

"Try? That's not good enough. Do. You've got to do."

"I was married. Bad loss and all that."

"Yes, I know. Sorry to hear it, old man. Help yourself to a smoke. On the table beside you."

Eric realized that Millardson had already checked into his personal life. He sipped at the Scotch uneasily. Being married was certainly an asset in conventional business circles, but not all that important. Hilda would have made a good impression, he thought with disgust.

"While we're having this little snort, let's find out who's available to entertain us." He leaped off the table and crossed to a sash hanging beside the maroon silk draperies. "One never knows what's prowling around this apartment. I woke up one morning with a tremendous urge to go horse back riding with my daughter Robin. She's a crackerjack with horses, better than her old man. So I got all spiffed up and knocked on the door. Three minutes later Alvie, that's my youngest, she comes marching by and says what are you doing there, Daddy? I tell her I'm going horse back riding with Robin. So she looks at me and bursts out laughing. If you want to go riding with Robin, she says, you better catch a plane to Havana. She left yesterday." He put his glass down, laughing the while to himself and shaking his head. "That's what I mean."

The maid came in with tiny silent steps. "Did you ring, sir?"

Millardson scratched the iron gray bristles of his hair. "Can you tell me who's in this blasted house tonight, Kate?"

Her pink and white complexion took on a puzzled look that spread up into her round blue eyes.

"Who's living here now? Since I'm only the father, I thought you'd know better than I do."

Kate swallowed, maintaining her trained smile. "I saw Master Donald early this afternoon, sir."

"Anyone else?"

She drew a breath, trying to think. "Well, Miss Alvie's gone away for the evening..."

"I didn't ask who's out. I want to know who's here. Now Donald, that's a pretty fair start. Is Robin in by any chance? Not that I expect her to be."

"Miss Robin is expected for supper, sir."

He took a long cigar from an inside pocket and snipped off the end of it with a tiny folding knife. "Don't tell me." He turned to Eric. "You're going to like Robin, my boy. She's all firecrackers."

"Will that be all, sir?"

"Yes. Thank you, Kate."

Kate executed a little curtsy and left.

"You can see who my favorite is," Millardson said. "Girls these days are so pallid. Sour cream. I dislike 'em thoroughly. But not my Robin. I hope she'll be along soon. But you can never tell about her."

Eric discovered he wasn't especially looking forward to an evening with Millardson's kids. He hoped it wasn't going to drag out to all hours. Cee-Zee alone. She might decide on another party. He shuddered privately, making a mental note to see what he could do about keeping business appointments during business hours. There was nothing in his contract that said he had to resign himself to the torture of playing potsy with family brats. He could imagine this Robin creature, oozing money and egomania. Maybe a young nympho or a sprouting junkie. He wanted to comment about how great it probably was to have a fine family but he couldn't cough out the crummy words. He watched Millardson puffing on the cigar and felt a wedge of pity for him. All the money in the world couldn't buy him freedom from this prison sentence imposed by the young Millardsons. He conjectured about whether the old guy might be carrying some kind of guilt that he was trying to atone for through his kids. The possible combinations of skeletons were infinite. But Eric didn't want to know the sob story. He had his own and that was plenty.

The bing-bong of the door floated into the room and Kate's little footsteps were heard on the marble.

"Your father's just been askin' for you." Her brogue lilted in to Eric. He saw Millardson cock his head.

The snicking sound of flat heeled leather shoes came toward them.

"That's my Robin," Millardson said. "Never get her out of those sandals. She was born wearing them."

Eric took a breath and prepared himself for the ordeal.

"Dad?"

Eric opened his eyes in the direction of the low melodious voice. He saw a young girl with auburn hair cut very short. Golden highlights shimmered in the strands pushed away from her high forehead. She moved toward Millardson, her black stretch pants not too tight, yet tight enough to shape the spare, resilient body. Black leather sandals clung to her feet as though she had indeed been born with them on. She kissed her father on the cheek and then turned to face Eric, unbuttoning the toggles of her cotton poplin jacket.

Instinctively Eric rose from his chair, smiling back at the sea-green eyes that focused on him.

"Robin, this is Eric Spokane who has come, in the guise of a friend, to do me out of a fortune of money."

She extended a hand to him with well-bred graciousness of a type one could never learn in a finishing school. "I hope you succeeed, Eric." Her smile revealed white teeth just the least bit uneven, which added a piquant interest to her mouth. The lipstick she wore was a pale orange, put on so very lightly that the color seemed a natural part of the lips, which turned up pixie-like at the corners.

Standing opposite her, he realized that she was much taller than he'd measured. Millardson reached just about up to her nose and he was beaming at her now.

"I'm glad you're not in Havana," Eric said.

She dropped her hands into her coat pockets, a faint blush tinging upward in her cheeks, but she did not drop her glance away from him. "Seems I have no more secrets," she said.

He thought that she must have lots of secrets and that he wouldn't mind finding all of them out for himself. Her nostrils flared slightly under his steady glance and he knew it would be polite to look away. But he didn't.

Millardson started to help her off with her coat, revealing a pearl gray sweater cable stitched in parallel lines over her round breasts, which stood up firmly beneath the light wool.

"Let's get you a drink," Millardson said, "now that you're legal."

"Dad means I'm twenty one," she said. "That was three weeks ago and he's been feeding me Gibsons ever since."

"Do you like them?" Eric said, feeding the conversation. Not giving a damn what they talked about so long as he could keep that lovely voice tuned in.

"Passable," she said. "But not for a serious drinker."

"All right, big girl," Millardson put in. "Name your weapons."

She looked at Eric and at the books and then at her father. "How about ginger ale?"

"On the rocks," Eric added.

"Yes."

Millardson glanced from one to the other of them. He was standing behind the cabinet bar, the cigar ash long and dangerously poised above the bucket of ice. "My daughter, for whom I have waited all these long years," he grunted around the thickness of the cigar. "Ginger ale."

But it was obvious that her reply pleased him. He took a crystal highball glass and dropped cubes into it, the clinking sound vibrating like bells.

She drank half of it thirstily, then peered at her watch. "I think I'll do something different tonight," she said.

Both Millardson and Eric waited silently.

"Dress for dinner." She beamed on her father with a special kindness that Eric could not name.

"Praise be," Millardson exclaimed.

"Will you both excuse me?"

"Certainly," Eric replied. He was very conscious that here was a girl who knew her own worth. It gave him the feeling of being very much alive. Though he was curious to see what she would consider being dressed for dinner, he also knew that he wouldn't care if she came to the table in a gunny sack.

When she had left, a tenseness which had unconsciously gripped him began to ebb.

"Now what do you say to my Robin?" Millardson stood complacently jiggling the ice cubes in his glass.

"I say congratulations," Eric replied mildly.

Privately he reflected that sometimes there could be certain compensations for business conducted after hours. He did not intend to persue any further interest in Robin than the casual pleasantries of tonight's meeting. It was a pity he hadn't run into her on a beach or in a bar someplace before he'd met Millardson. In these circumstances, however, it would not be to his advantage, mixing private life with business. No doubt the doting father had plans for his lovely offspring. And he didn't blame Millardson. The percentage of worthwhile females was small enough. And here was one who definitely deserved the best. She should have a guy with something to give besides the usual kicks. For the first time in a long while, he felt used up, shabby. Whatever he'd been born with in the way of decent emotions was long since worn away. He wondered if this was how Cee-Zee felt. As he thought about her, he began to sense an inkling of understanding. Those unpredictable moods, the desire to trade herself for the superficial security of a marriage to someone like Lilio. The more he thought about Cee-Zee, the more he felt their strange comradeship.

But for tonight, he would allow himself to enjoy Robin. He would be a bystander at the spectacle.

"It won't take her long to dress," Millardson commented.

He nodded, expecting that whatever Robin's failings were, they would not become apparent on first meeting. His primary reason for coming tonight was beginning to take second place in his thoughts. With an effort, Eric hauled himself away from musing about Robin. He started to figure an opening maneuver about the account.

But Millardson was apparently in no mood to discuss finances. Already on his third drink, he felt even more than usually expansive about his children and he made no attempt to dilute it with topics that could more easily include Eric.

"Now that you've met the best of my lot," he said, "you can gear yourself to meeting the worst. And mind you, I'm just as fond of Donald. In a different way, of course."

Millardson needed to talk. It was not to Eric's advantage to interrupt him. But the reappearance of Kate saved Eric.

"The blasted supper can wait," Millardson said good-naturedly. He looked up to meet the girl's helpless expression. "All right. We'll come in."

Eric followed them through a long maze of foyer, overly decorated with arrangements of mirrors that caught and reflected light painfully. He wondered which of the family was so interested in looking at himself or herself. They came into a large dining room dominated by deep green panels of silk, green curtains and a green rug that blended with the mahogany table. The room did not feel conducive to eating and he got the feeling somehow that Millardson must often dine here alone.

"Sit down. Sit down. Robin'll be with us in a minute, if I know her."

And he had hardly finished the sentence when she came in again.

She certainly had changed, Eric thought, staring with bad manners at the pale yellow dress which made her eyes a deep emerald. It fell softly over her body, tantalizing him by implying the shape of her beneath it. As she moved, he could tell a soft curve of breast, the narrowing line of ribs as these outlines came and went in shadow. She seemed quite unaware of her body. Only the pink-white shoulders were naked. They seemed untouched. He could not really believe that she might be a virgin. Her very innocence was tremulous like the climbing of passion. A string of tiny pearls dipped into the curve of her throat, but other than that she wore no jewelry. Her slim arms were bare, her fingers too except for the gloss of natural polish outlining the ovals and the very white disks extending slightly beyond the tips of her fingers.

Behind her loomed an extremely tall man, almost paper thin. He did not seem to have the strength to hold his spine erect. He bore a caricature resemblance to Robin. Her auburn hair was carrot red on him. And the green eyes had become a watery gray.

"Hello again," Eric said, ignoring the man and speaking directly to Robin.

"Hello," she said softly, reaching behind her and taking the man's hand. "This is my brother Donald." She made the introductions casually.

Eric stepped forward to shake Donald's hand.

"You came on a good night," Donald said from between overlapping teeth. "Robin isn't always here so we can look at her. She is pretty, isn't she? I don't blame you for staring at her. We all wish we could more often." His voice was oddly high, as though part of him had forgotten to go through puberty. As he stood close to Eric, a fine yellow fuzz was visible on his cheeks indicating that he never shaved.

Eric felt himself stiffen. He waited for Robin to stop holding Donald's hand. But instead, she led him to the chair beside her own.

"All right, kids, break it up," Millardson laughed uneasily. "Does anyone know who else might be joining us?"

"I think we're complete," Robin offered. She looked across directly at Eric. "I hope you aren't too disappointed."

"Not at all."

"Why should he be?" Donald took his napkin and shook out the folds.

"Your brother's right," Eric said.

Kate rolled in a tray crowded with tureens and Eric subsided into silence. He wondered how far Robin went in pampering her brother.

Millardson took over the conversation, directing it back to his second favorite topic of horses. Many platters of food came and went. Eric managed to salvage his appetite in spite of Donald. Putting mental blinders on, he concentrated on the glowing Robin, allowing himself occasionally to accept Millardson into his range of view.

"I wanted one of my boys to be a jockey, except that I never got a son in the right proportions."

"We're a gambling family," Donald said. "You've still got time."

"That we are. That we are. I don't suppose you do much betting on the horses, Eric?"

"Not any more. I like a sport where the odds are a little bit more maneuverable."

"And what would that be?" Donald ran his bony fingers through his hair in a weak imitation of his father's habitual gesture.

Eric was about to say women but changed his mind. "There are lots."

"For example?" Robin questioned with an honest curiosity that amused him. He decided at that moment that she must be a virgin.

"Oh, cards, for example."

"You're not a poker player?" Millardson said.

"Yes. A little."

"I guess that's all right if you win. Do you win?"

"I've been winning." He moved the serrated edges of his steak knife slowly through the meat, watching the juice ooze and not wanting to look to see if Robin approved or disapproved. They made an interesting trio, this father and his two so-called children. Donald could be anywhere from nineteen to thirty five. And Robin was the kind who would look seventeen forever. Their personalities seemed to intermingle, making an odd family brew that he would rather have avoided. It seemed inevitable that Millardson had distasteful memories. And, too, it seemed inevitable that Millardson would have to talk about them. Not tonight perhaps. Not next week. But sooner or later. Eric felt that the man was going to get drunk and corner him with the burden of his story. Perhaps he was saving the contract for such a time, unconsciously tying Eric to him by dangling the sweet plum of his account until he had relieved himself of whatever incredible history haunted him. Uneasily Eric stirred in his seat, not sure that his commission was worth it, feeling that he wanted no part of Millardson's past and certainly no part of his future except for the signing of his name on a certain dotted line.

"Donald plays poker," Robin said.

"You're mistaken, my dear. I only watch the game." His thin blonde eyebrows moved nervously on the bony ridge of his skull. "I don't care to be involved." He twirled the stem of the sherry glass in front of him. "To become involved is so…"

He did not stop for lack of the right word, but rather because he did not wish to use it, Eric thought.

"... dirty," Eric said.

"Yes." His pale lips widened a little. The ends of his mouth seemed to dissolve away in his fleshless cheeks. "We must talk sometime, you and I."

Not if I can avoid it, Eric thought. He glanced over to see how Millardson was taking all this and saw that he had relapsed into his sixth whiskey. But the alcohol had not touched his senses. The eyes remained bright and alert. Eric realized that Millardson had been watching him all this while to see how he was evaluating his children.

He struggled through the parfait dessert, avoiding conclusions in his own head about Donald. What troubled him most of all was Robin. She did not seem to mind her brother. He did not affect her. If anything, her protective attitude encouraged him. Eric wondered how long she could go on encouraging him without getting caught in something too distasteful even for Robin's innocence.

In comparsion with all this, Cee-Zee seemed remarkably uncomplicated. He tried to think about her to refresh himself with something familiar. He recalled lying between her legs, the short sounds escaping her wet mouth. He recalled when she sighed: Spooky, you're hurting me. The blunt, predictable action of sex was something he longed for right now in the company of these people who seemed to avoid it, substituting he knew not what perversions of the natural climax.

"Shall we go into the library?" Donald said. He got up and held the chair back for his sister, not touching her with his hands but working his gaze over the outline of her rounded shoulders and downward into the crevice of her gown.

Eric's hand balled into a fist at his side. It could not be that Robin was this unaware of her brother. Yet she smiled and swept up from her seat, refusing a cigarette from her father as though Donald's staring did not exist.

"If you'll excuse me," she said, "I must go upstairs for awhile."

"Letters again?" Donald exclaimed, his voice a trifle higher. "You're going to wear your pen out and that beautiful arm."

She smiled at him. "I'll be down as soon as I can."

Eric stood still until she had gone, cursing the fact that it wasn't Donald who had letters to write. Then he returned with Millardson to the library where Donald took away the pool cues and set up the triangle. He did not invite anyone to play with him but went slowly through the ritual of hitting the balls, playing with sleepy movements that belied his tremendous ability.

"You're a patient man, Eric," Millardson said, rolling the glass he had brought with him between his palms. "I hope I don't try your patience much further."

"You underestimate your friend," Donald said.

Eric wasn't quite sure that this was a compliment but he let Donald's words pass.

"To tell you the truth, I like to avoid business as much as possible. Frankly, I don't give a damn about this insurance. My factories could burn down over night and I'd still have more money than one man could spend in a lifetime."

Eric was not quite so patient as Donald had expected. "Just as frankly, Martin, why am I here?" He accepted another Scotch and set it on the table without tasting it.

"My account could mean a lot of money to someone without it being any skin off my nose. I realize that and I want to do something..."

"Philanthropic," Donald put in.

Eric felt himself getting angry.

"Uh uh," Millardson raised his hand, anticipating Eric's reply. "Donald said that. I didn't."

"Well, just what is it, then?" Eric said. He wanted to cut this short before getting involved. Already he could see the growing signs of expansiveness returning in Millardson. He had a way of squaring his shoulders and taking a deep breath as though he were preparing to jump from a great height.

"My reasons are pretty involved."

To hell with your reasons, Eric thought. Do we get it or don't we?

"I know you don't want me to go into details. You don't strike me as a very patient man, Eric, despite Donald's observation. You're a getter, Eric. I used to be one too. I think Robin is."

"But not your son?" Donald looked up from his bent position over the cue.

"That's right. Not my son." Millardson's words were clipped. His camouflage of pride was beginning to crack now, not under the pressure of alcohol but because Donald himself was so obviously nothing one could fool a stranger about.

There was a knock on the door and Kate came in. She was carrying a red telephone on a long wire.

"It's for Mr. Spokane," she said.

Eric excused himself, unable to hide his surprise. Kate put the phone on the table beside the wing chair and he stood with the receiver.

"It's me, Spooky. I just had a terrific idea. And since you left your date book near the phone, I couldn't help seeing it. Why don't you meet me on the corner of Fifty Third and Third and we'll go to Lilio's place. That way he can see we're all friends again."

Eric glanced at his watch. It was already past eleven. "I can't make it definite."

"But you said between eleven and twelve."

"I know, I know. Look, why don't I just pick you up at the house so you don't have to wait on the street?"

"You don't fool me. It'll be hours before you drag yourself away. You're worse than an old woman."

"I'll phone you when I'm ready to leave." He cradled the receiver, hoping she wouldn't think he was hanging up on her and phone back again.

"At least *you* aren't celibate," Millardson said after Kate had left.

Eric looked at him narrowly.

"Come along," Millardson continued. "We're all men in this room. At least I think we are."

"My beloved father believes that women are either mothers or whores," Donald said. "I'll make it simple for you, Eric, so that you can leave in time for your appointment." He stood the cue on its wide end and rested his hands on the tip. "My father is convinced that some willing, and clean, woman should be employed for the purpose of initiating his eldest son into the animal delights of intercourse."

He's damned right, Eric thought.

"But, you see, he is also afraid to do the procuring for me because of a vulgar little complication known as blackmail. Therefore, if he can find a bright gentleman willing to act as a middleman, he would make it very worth his while."

"By giving him an insurance contract," Eric finished. He looked to Millardson for denial and found the man watching with controlled anxiousness.

Millardson took off his glasses and wiped them cautiously. "I'm sure you realize that it's not as simple as it sounds, Eric. But *you* can make it simple. I have made it my business to find out about you—or, more precisely, your women. They aren't the ordinary run. And that's what interests me."

The implications of Millardson's statement filled the silence. Eric thought, So the old boy figures Donald can't make it with an ordinary whore. He's convinced the kid needs something special and that I can supply it. And will, if the price is right.

He felt a great surge to say: you can both go to hell. What stopped him was the recollection of Donald looking down his sister's dress. The possibility that he would someday be alone in the house with his sister, or anywhere alone with her .... It would be one thing if she were properly careful, if she could understand that her brother's desires were centering on her own body. No doubt she would think anyone crazy who tried to caution her.

Eric buttoned his jacket and took a final cigarette from the table case. He saw the old man waiting expectantly. He supposed that Millardson too was aware of Donald's potential action. "All right, Martin," he said. "I'll give it some thought."

His tacit agreement made the room almost bearable.

CHAPTER FIVE

Instead of phoning Cee-Zee, he went back to the apartment for her. The combination of Donald and Lilio both in one evening! Too much. He wanted to be alone with Cee-Zee for awhile. Strip off the fancy suit and chase her around the bedroom.

He put the key in the lock and found that the door was open. The sound of cha-cha music blasted him. He stood at the living room entrance and watched unnoticed. She was wiggling her hips and snapping her fingers, eyes half closed, lips pursed in private enjoyment. Eric folded his arms and leaned aagnsit the wall, not wanting to disturb the picture. She had on a black velvet dress that left her back completely naked down to the waist, revealing the movement of her shoulder blades and the snake-like suppleness of her spine. Her buttocks poked out like an African native. He viewed its arching movements with appreciation. She whirled on her skyscraper heels and stopped abruptly, catching sight of him. Then she laughed soundlessly and danced over toward him. He put his arm around her and grasped one half of her behind, stepping with her now in time to the music. Their bodies meshed as she lifted her hips toward him and she darted the point of her tongue across his lips. As they passed the radio, she reached out and snapped it off, ducking out of his arms.

He grabbed for her but she swivelled away. "Mustn't mess the merchandise. Besides, you were supposed to phone."

"Yeah, and you weren't."

"Did I louse you up, I hope?" She tightened one pendant earring of sparkling amethyst.

"No, sweetie, you'll have to try again." He nodded toward the earrings and the dress. "I see you didn't waste any time spending your salary."

"And we're not going to waste any more time sexing around here, so cool your irons."

"You were pretty anxious this afternoon."

"Tch, tch. The mating season is over. We're going out on *my* business appointment. You're about to see an after hours joint that makes ordinary screwing look like its out of style. My knight in flabby armor has to be respected for one thing. He knows how to keep his clientele from getting bored. Besides, you'll meet all the best people. Isn't that what you like?"

He was more interested in finding out how she kept her breasts up in the two v-shaped pieces of material. The flesh jiggled as she spoke, threatening to fall out any moment. A heavy fragrance rose from her soft cleavage. He bent over and put his nose into it. "We can go tomorrow," his words came muffled from her skin.

She put her hands over his ears and lifted his head away. "You're supposed to be my friend."

He remembered, all of a sudden, the pact he'd made with himself about Cee-Zee. No forcing, no cajoling. "Well, what happens when we get there?"

"Oh, you won't be ignored," she laughed. "Plenty of licks and kicks for all. Strictly adult entertainment guaranteed."

It occurred to him that there might be something he could take home for Donald.

"Promise one thing, Spooky. Be nice to me while we're there. I want to get Lilio good and jealous. And if you can't be nice, be real awful so he'll feel sorry for me and want to protect me."

"That's my girl, all curves and angles."

He waited while she went to fetch a matching velvet purse and stole, draping it around her shoulders so that the white satin lining folded over her arms. The characteristic easiness which had been a gratifying part of him during the past year was gone. In the past few days something had begun to force it away. A driving urge toward violence which had taken full control of him for an instant with Hilda. The muscles in his jaw flicked. He couldn't see himself. That his posture had taken a compact stance, bracing for an explosion. Something of a pallor seeped beneath his olive skin. His neck had thickened with a bulge of tendon. But all this was imperceptible to any casual observer. All he knew was that he was beginning to lose patience with people trying to make a revolving door of his private life.

They went out again and rode over to the West Side, speeding through Central Park. The cool rustling of shadowed trees was louder to him than the whine of the tires. He didn't talk much. He didn't feel like wise cracking with her. His legs were stiff and cold, his body felt rigid also. The sense of well-being, of suppleness replaced by a steel tube that held his guts in place.

Lilio's club was stashed in the basement of an old brownstone. They got to it through a series of passages fumigated to kill the smell of sewage.

"This better be good," he commented.

Before he had a chance to find out whether it was good or not, he realized that it certainly was interesting.

The huge low-ceilinged room was lit by a series of blue lights just bright enough to reveal the waitresses, each clad in a tiny gauze apron, flesh-tinted panties and a pair of rosebuds.

"This is the tired business man's appetizer," Cee-Zee murmured as she searched around the room for Lilio.

"Then maybe we better have a drink," Eric said. "Let's grab that table."

He caught the eye of one of the waitresses. She wiggled her way to them between the crowded chairs.

"Two Scotch on the rocks."

When she brought them, Eric pulled out a couple of bills and dropped them on the ash tray.

She smiled pleasantly enough, her white bleached hair falling forward over her shoulders.

"Keep the change," Eric said.

As she walked away, he watched her pink behind wiggling and dimpling beneath the huge pussy cat bow of her apron ties.

"The fate of the working girl," Eric grinned.

"And last winter, Geraldine was clerking for a credit jeweler," Cee-Zee added.

"You know her?"

"Obviously, shnook."

"Pardon me."

"Maybe I better go ask her if Lilio's busy inside."

"Yeah, let's go inside. This is strictly for tourists," he said, following her between the tables.

They reached Geraldine as she was bending over, shoving her collection of tips into the side of one shoe.

"You want to go back stage?" she said, looking up.

Cee-Zee nodded.

"Who's the beefcake?"

"Blood cousin," Eric said. "Pleased to meet you."

"He's always snotty," Cee-Zee put in. "That's all the charm he's got."

Geraldine rose to her full five feet one. "He looks like he might have something more."

"You're all right too, little girl. If you ever want to work overtime, let me know."

"Come on, flip lip," Cee-Zee said.

They wangled around behind the bar and bent down to get through a small door. Lilio was standing just on the other side of it, his fat belly obstructing the entrance. His plastered down hair gave off a rancid odor meant to be masculine perfume. He lifted a warning finger to his lips and motioned them to a table against the wall.

Only half a dozen people were in this room and none of them paid any attention to the disturbance of Cee-Zee and Eric. The reason for this was a girl in a sequined bikini, rocking on her knees in the middle of the circle. Sitting on the floor beside her was a chimpanzee trying to peel a banana. She was making cooing sounds at the chimp, attempting to distract his attention by slapping her thighs and leaning toward him. Occasionally the chimp would glance at her. But always, his attention returned to the food in his mind.

Eric looked around to see that both men and women at the various tables were desperately involved with whether the food or the girl would finally win the chimp.

"Come on, Adam," one of the men rooted drunkenly. "You ain't that hungry."

Lilio said, "Five minutes, forty three seconds."

"There's a time limit and she's not allowed to touch him," Cee-Zee whispered. "That's what makes the suspense."

"What happens if she loses?"

"You'll see."

Eric crossed his legs and expelled a long breath. "How much of this do we have to go through before you make your impression on Lilio?"

Cee-Zee frowned without answering him.

Meanwhile the chimp had edged closer to the girl and was now leaping up and down, the banana half peeled, biting into it contentedly as though he were all alone with it.

"Three minutes, twenty nine seconds," Lilio announced.

Excitedly the girl clapped her hands in front of Adam's nose. But he rubbed his eyes, dropped the banana skin and waddled away.

"Smart cookie," Eric whispered.

Now all the men started to lean over. "Here, Adam." They snapped their fingers and put glasses of water on the floor, banging the glasses with knives or forks.

Adam stopped, bewildered by all the noise. He scratched his head and yawned, curling back his upper lip in what seemed to be a superior laugh. Then he sat down and rolled over, one arm curling around his neck.

Eric lit a cigarette and yawned too, letting the smoking match fall to the floor.

Of all things, it was this match which attracted Adam's attention. He leaped over and squatted beside Eric's foot. Then he reached out a hand and caught his trousers cuff, pulling it and screeching.

Cee-Zee burst into a roar of laughter. "You're it," she squealed. "Spooky won the package."

He watched her double over in fits of uncontrollable giggling. Then he looked about, very sure that he didn't want to find out the cause of her hysterics.

Lilio came over and hoisted the chimp into his arms. He patted Eric's shoulder. "Ah, monsieur is most fortunate," he said. "Adam has chosen you to take his place. Bon voyage."

Eric looked from Lilio to Cee-Zee to the girl lying on the floor. He put his hands up. "Oh, no," he said. "I'm just a bystander."

"You do not wish to …"

"Mus' be a fag," someone shouted drunkenly; interrupting Lilio.

Eric stood up, the chair toppling backward from his movement.

"He ain't no fag," Cee-Zee shouted back.

She reached forward to grab his belt buckle. He caught her wrist and twisted it away. "Take it easy, kid," he said from between grim lips.

Eric flung Cee-Zee away from him. She fell back against the chair.

"*You* take it easy," Lilio's voice came out breathily. His eyes seemed to sink deeper into the rolls of fat as they became pin points of anger.

The drunk wavered forward, tottering toward Eric. But the flashing sequins attracted his eye. He hiccoughed and flopped down on the floor beside the girl. "Not nice to fight in the presence of ladies," he mumbled, tangling his fingers in her flame red hair.

"You better get out, monsieur." The bland camoflage had dropped completely. The chimp hugged Lilio, bouncing up and down in the crook of his elbow.

Eric's arm came up and he whacked Lilio across the face with the back of his hand. He knew the insult of this was more sickening than any punch. The round, oily face became hard, menacing.

"Watch yourself," Lilio's voice was a whisper. "You be in trouble now, monsieur."

"Go to hell."

Eric strode out, leaving Cee-Zee with Lilio.

Ducking through the door, he searched for Geraldine and found her skimmering through the crowd, holding a tray of glasses high above her head, her pendulous breasts slapping as she walked. He waited beside the bar until she served the liquor and returned.

"Hi," she said. "Where's your girl friend?"

"You want to make some more money for that shoe?" he asked, ignoring her question.

Geraldine shrugged.

"I mean real money. Say a couple of hundred for a night's engagement."

"That's a lot of money, mister."

He figured Millardson wouldn't think so. "Give me your phone number and you'll find out."

"I work for Lilio."

"No free-lance, eh?"

He let her inspect him until she was satisfied that he wasn't kidding. Then she came close and whispered her number into his ear. "Mornings only," she said.

"Check."

He left the place thinking that Donald would consider her a poor substitute for Robin. Yet Geraldine had her points. He didn't doubt that she had the know-how to give Donald whatever perverted kicks he might require.

When he got home, the apartment seemed peculiarly empty. He took some ginger ale from the refrigerator and added gin to it, promising himself that if Cee-Zee came back, he'd kick her down the steps. She wanted her Lilio. Now she had him. He looked hopefully around to see if, by any chance, she had forgotten to take the key with her. He didn't want Cee-Zee bouncing in any time of the day or night. It made him feel helpless to know all the hours during the week he'd be stuck at the office, leaving her free to come and to do as she pleased.

He saw a pair of her soiled underpanties stuffed into a corner of the couch and he jammed them into the garbage can beneath the sink. What burned him more than anything was the way she'd played along with the drunk. It was a small but traitorous action which clued him into the fact that Cee-Zee was hopelessly no good. He must have been some kind of crazy to consider helping her. From now on, he promised himself, dames would be dames for him and nothing else.

He sank down onto the couch and found his mind idling in the sea green mist of Robin's eyes. He shut the thought off with a violent snap.

The telephone began to ring.

At this hour it could only be Cee-Zee. He let it ring on, counting the limits of her patience. It stopped for awhile and then began again. He got up and went to the phone, unscrewed the mouthpiece to stop the buzz, and put the receiver under his pillow.

CHAPTER SIX

The ringing of the telephone became the ringing of the doorbell, waking him from a light doze on the couch. He scratched an itch in the stubble beneath his chin and his eyes squinted open. The doorbell kept ringing insistently, echoing through his head. He sat up out of the patch of morning sunlight and got to his feet. He had fallen asleep dressed. He looked down to see the bags and creases in his trousers as he wandered, still not awake, to open the door. Cee-Zee, anybody would be better than the blasted ringing that stabbed through his temples.

He groped for the door knob and turned it. "You? What the deuce are you doing here?" This was just what he didn't need, Hilda in the middle of everything.

She stood on the threshold, her startled eyes examining him mutely as he turned and walked away from her back to the couch. "I've been trying to call you since yesterday. Your line has been busy for twenty four hours. I tried to get the operator to help me. I began to worry. And now I see that I was right. What's happened to you, Eric? Look at yourself."

She stood over him, her gloved hands clutching her purse, her voice concerned, yet harsh with judgment.

"The telephone was as good an excuse as any, eh, Hilda?" He spoke without opening his eyes.

"What do you mean?"

"I mean you're bugging me, girl. Why don't you just go away." He didn't have the strength to be kind or tactful. The mistake of going to her place was beginning to snowball. But if she thought she could get hooks into him again because they'd spent a few hours together, she was damn well mistaken.

She lay her purse on the table and began to pull her gloves off slowly, one finger at a time. "You know I won't take that kind of talk from anybody. Be civil at least, Eric. I didn't come with a shotgun."

"Why not? I could use a shotgun or a shot or something. As long as you're here, why don't you make yourself useful? The whiskey's in the cabinet over the sink."

He heard her breath draw in. If she were smart, she'd realize there was nothing he could give her except a hard time. She might realize it all right, but she wouldn't admit it. Not to herself or to him. He felt sad for her and sadder for himself because of the bastard he became in her presence, automatically.

"Well, go on already," he said, wishing there was a quicker way of death for Hilda then this slow bleeding.

She didn't answer him but he heard her footsteps moving and the click of the cabinet doors. A slave, a pretty little Oriental slave. He never could understand why she needed this. Yet maybe it was true that some women worked that way. Love and all that crap, or maybe the first man who took their virginity became a god. The thought tasted rotten.

Hilda came back with a glass one third full of Scotch. He sat up and rubbed his calves, then took the glass. "Thanks."

"If I didn't feel so sorry for you…"

"Can it." He took a swallow and put the glass down on the rug. "Feel sorry for me, my foot. You came here looking for a lay. You must've been damn glad the telephone gave you the excuse. Stop blinking those shocked eyes at me. There's too much going on as it is and I don't need more aggravation from you."

He saw that her hands were trembling. She walked around to the back of an empty chair and leaned against it. Her glance could not meet his.

"I don't know what to say to you," she choked.

"Then it's simple. Don't say anything." He took up the glass again and finished its contents.

"You're the cruelest person I've ever known." Her mouth pursed hard, fighting not to give way to tears.

"Meat balls." He had to keep hitting and hitting at her. He pulled open the bow tie and dragged it out from the collar. Then he took off his jacket and tossed it on the chair against which she was leaning.

"How frightening you seem," she went on. "Like an animal. Those red eyelids, those rumpled clothes. I don't know how you live like this, Eric, after what you've become accustomed to."

He continued unbuttoning his shirt, dropping it carelessly on the floor. "Did I ask you for a gold star? If you came by to see if I was all right, you see it. Now why don't you be a good little girl and scram? I've got lots to do today."

She came around to pick up his shirt to put it beside his jacket. "I'm not sure that I do see you are all right. If anything, I'd say that you're all wrong. Do you want to talk about it, dear? I know how it is when you have fits of temper like this. And perhaps I shouldn't blame you."

He moved his hand into the opening of her dress and squeezed the cup of her brassiere. "You want talk?" he said. "You want to hear my troubles, is that it?"

With a weak gesture, she pretended to try to move his hand away. He held on tight, undoing the snaps of her blouse with the other hand.

"You're not very convincing," he said.

"Oh, Eric." She fell against him, the sobs coming warm onto his chest. "You don't know the torture. You just don't know." Hot tears trembled down his chest. "I've tried so hard. Did you think I wanted to come to you? This way, like a beggar. What do you think it does to a woman's pride when she can't stay away from someone? I wasn't brought up to understand this. And I don't know how to cope with it now. Darling, I'm pleading with you.

Please have mercy. Sometimes I think I'm going out of my mind. The awful dreams. My mind is a wild thing. Ever since you left me ... the dizziness ... the needing you. What can I say? And that Friday night. I should have ignored you. But I couldn't. I couldn't let you get away without touching you. Please. Be kind. I won't bother you too often. I promise that. Just once in a while, let me hold you, kiss you. I'll be anything for you. Do anything. Only you mustn't throw me away."

She clung to him fiercely, her ribs panting fast, strands of hair smeared in perspiration across her forehead, the odor of her perfume mingling with the faint tinge of desire that rose from her body with a fragrance of its own.

As he remained silent, she lifted her face after awhile, trying to smile blearily through her make-up. "It's your fault, after all," she said. "You taught me how."

There was no answer for her. Gently he disengaged her hands from behind him. What would it cost, in the long run, if he took care of Hilda's desire every so often? He knew her well enough not to give in right away. She could get to be a problem if he let her believe she could sway him. Her demands would not stop after bed. Pretty soon, she'd be asking him to escort her to parties, involving him again in the whirl of social life he hated.

"Please, say you won't turn me away." Her dress had slopped down off her shoulders. A sliver of brassiere strap glistened in the sunlight. "I know what you're thinking," she added hurriedly. "And I promise not to become a nuisance. Really. I swear on my life that I won't ask more than a few hours from you. After all," she said bitterly, "a woman knows when the man she loves doesn't love her in return."

"As long as that's clear," he said.

"Yes." She put the tips of her fingers on his lips. "I would turn the world inside out if I thought it could change you. But I know better."

He sat down onto the couch bringing her with him on his lap. Her hot mouth opened his lips. The flat width of her tongue reached in greedily. She turned in his arms and hoisted her skirt, straddling his lap. Her garters glinted on the hem of her stockings. Her belly began undulating against him. Despite himself, arrows of response began shooting through him. The energies of last night, energies meant for Cee-Zee, converged in his loins. Her small school teacher's hands reached beneath his belt, massaging him. She edged herself forward, her spread legs stretching her thin girdle wide. Deftly she unhooked the garters. The girdle rolled up over her hips.

"Darling, hurry," she moaned, forgetting the mask of prudishness, all of her concentrating on one thing as she bumped herself against him.

He didn't have to do anything but let her unzip him. She drew in her breath, her mouth placid, her tongue lolling out. Her eyes became dull with a familiar glaze.

He surrendered to the wet caressing touch of her lips. All his muscles tightened and the throbbing in his head became a complete throbbing of his body.

She sat up and shimmied her hips down, groaning with the contact. He felt her expand as they moved in rhythm.

"So good," she murmured, not realizing that she was speaking.

She leaned her forehead against the back of the couch, all of her moving violently, insistently. Now and then she shuddered in a series of convulsions that clutched her whole body but she did not stop the pounding of her hips against him. Beads of sweat ran down her arms, staining the material of her dress. And still she pivoted on him, all of her wracked with tortured seeking of completion.

He felt himself burst and he gripped her down to him, his fingers digging into her shoulders. Her answering response made all of her vibrate in a final ecstasy.

She fell away from him, her wet face relaxed. Limply she lay with her eyes closed, ignoring the rumpled skirt and girdle tangled about her waist.

Now she didn't need words, she didn't need to plead with him. He stood up and went to wash his face, thinking how in these times afterward, she must hate him.

When he returned from the bathroom, she still hadn't moved. But now she opened her eyes, smiling weakly, the lip stick a pink smudge across her upper lip. "There can't be anyone else quite so wonderful," she said.

He looked at her curving belly, the pale fuzz on it moving with the rhythm of her breathing. He wished she would fix her clothes but he didn't find it necessary to comment. Let her enjoy the few moments for what they were worth to her.

Going into the bathroom, he changed his rumpled trousers, pulling on a pair of old army fatigues. If he were lucky, she'd go away soon and he could spend a nice quiet time alone for a change.

He had just pulled a polo shirt over his head when he heard a key in the lock. He ran to intercept Cee-Zee before she got to the living room.

Catching her at the door, he started to yank her with him back into the hall. But the slow light in her eyes told him it was too late. Still, he didn't want Hilda to have to face this. The humiliation would be too much. He got Cee-Zee by her biceps and forced her outside, slamming the door shut between themselves and Hilda.

She had changed into a green linen dress and all of her was put together with the loving care of a sleek, custom made automobile. He held her against the wall until he was sure she wouldn't try to get back inside the apartment. Standing this close to her, he could see beneath the make-up to the bluish circles under her eyes. Obviously she was not as well cared for and rested as she wanted to appear. This gratified him with a razor's edge of satisfaction.

"Now let's have the key," he said. "You're through with this place. Go on home to Lilio. Give him your snow jobs."

"First get those sweaty hands off me. And second, here's five dollars. Go buy yourself a sense of humor."

He looked at her hard and saw that she wasn't angry nor was she rebellious. A hint of disappointment shimmered in her eyes. His satisfaction fizzled.

"Anyway," she continued, "I came over to let you know what's happening and to thank you. By being your naturally ugly self, you did me a big favor. Lilio got me a place, since obviously I can't stay with you anymore. All the trimmings go with it. He's going to support me in the style to which he thinks I am accustomed." She sighed with amusement. "As for you, King Kong, Lilio's got his chubby little fighting feathers prickled. I'll do my best to take his mind off you. But have a care. One never knows when I may have to submit to your hospitality again and I don't like to share digs with the rigor mortis type. Too smelly."

She spoke with an honest concern for him. All his anger for Cee-Zee spilled over. In its stead, he felt a wave of admiration for her sportsmanship. Any other woman would be on her high horse or reduced to tears. Try to get even with him in some way. But Cee-Zee took it all without hard feelings. He might not agree with the way she lived, but there was no doubting the fact that he liked her despite everything.

She dropped the key into his hand. "I didn't mean to barge in on you. Go back to your friend." She turned and went down the hallway to the stairs.

As she started down them, Hilda came out. She had fixed her clothes and her make-up. But her eyes were wild with the attempt to keep her humiliation in control.

Mercifully Cee-Zee didn't look up but continued down the stairwell.

He pushed Hilda back inside.

She wanted to say something but her lips could not form the words.

"You don't have to worry," Eric said. "Nobody's going to tell on you." If it had been Cee-Zee caught on the couch instead of Hilda, she would have laughed and invited the intruder in.

Hilda's face was a deadly pallor.

"Oh, come on, relax. You're not the Queen of Sheba."

"I'm not… anybody," she said in a thin voice. "Just a tramp off the streets."

"Can't you quit the melodrama? Nobody's accusing you of anything." He put the key on a table, almost sorry now that Cee-Zee had given it back to him.

"Who is she?" Hilda looked at him furtively. She took a cigarette and put it between her lips.

"A friend. Just an old friend," he answered tiredly. "Don't ask me to explain. You'd never understand it."

She waited for Eric to strike a match for her. He went to the window and pulled the shades up instead. Anything he might tell her about Cee-Zee would sound like lies.

"Any woman who has a key to a man's apartment is surely a friend." Her voice was hardly above a whisper. "I know I have no claims on you, Eric, darling…"

"Then let it go at that." He spat the words out angrily. He wished it were Cee-Zee crawling to him like this instead of Hilda.

"I only hope I didn't spoil anything. Between you and that woman, I mean. Maybe she didn't expect you to be… busy this morning. Maybe my presence here will upset her. Women are jealous cats, you know."

He laughed in her face and Hilda looked at him, her mouth dry, her eyes large with bewilderment.

"That bitch jealous?" A taste of bitterness filled him.

For a moment Hilda remained silent, watching his reaction with an eagle alertness. She got her own match and struck it. Then she sat down and crossed her legs, tugging her skirt carefully over her knees. "You're rather impressed with her, aren't you, dear," she said quietly.

"The hell I am!" He was looking down into the backyard, watching some children on their tricycles.

"I never saw any one woman enrage you like that."

"We don't have to talk about it." He didn't mean to have Hilda dissecting his affairs. He certainly would not have her throwing fits of jealousy. Not because of Cee-Zee, of all people. The whole thing was too stupid. He felt helpless and irritable. He wished he could dig up a card game where the stakes were so high that he could win himself a year's freedom from all those silly female capers running in circles around him. He remembered Millardson's story about Robin hopping off to Cuba. That was one advantage to being a rich bitch. He wondered if Robin had anything to run away from. If she did, she kept it well hidden.

Thoughts of freedom and thoughts of summer intermingled with the grim reminder that he would have only a two week vacation. The chains of his every day job felt suddenly heavy. He couldn't see himself putting on a shirt and jacket and tie in the muggy heat. There was something foolish and inhuman about it.

"You're very quiet," Hilda said.

He had forgotten her presence momentarily. "I was thinking about July and August," he sighed. "And that reminds me, I have some work to prepare for tomorrow. I could use a little privacy, if you don't mind."

"How dare I mind?" She smiled sadly. "You never told me about your job though. Do you enjoy it?"

She was stalling for time. He wanted to tell her that this was no way to make him feel closer to her. He got her purse and gloves and handed them over.

"So so," he said. He lifted her up off the couch and walked her to the door.

"You'll phone me so I won't have to worry about busy signals?"

"Sure."

She tilted her face for a goodbye kiss. He pecked her on the forehead and got her out the door, shutting it fast before she thought of some new excuse to come back inside.

Alone now, he could let himself think about Cee-Zee without having to watch his expression for Hilda's sake. Impressed with her? Hilda should only know how very much impressed with her he really was. It was a strange kind of feeling utterly alien to him. She was something elusive, almost mysterious in her own vague way. Too rotten for any man, yet certainly too good for Lilio. He could imagine her throwing his money around for toys. She wasn't the kind to save any for hard times. Squander a fortune in a month. Then starve for half a year. For all her plotting to keep safe access to Lilio's bank account, she wouldn't have the consistency or the self control not to get rid of him as soon as he jangled her nerves. He expected that, pretty soon, she would be coming round again for his key. Just a matter of waiting it out.

CHAPTER SEVEN

He moved restlessly around his apartment, telling himself it was good to be alone. There were loose ends that had to be tied up. First of all, the situation with Millardson and his far out son. This was probably not the first time Millardson had tried to work out a deal about Donald. Eric began to consider the gimmicks so they wouldn't snap shut in his face. He had to know Donald better. Anticipate his reactions. Discover his weaknesses. He didn't like the idea much. But in order not to mess things up, he had to get Donald talking. Maybe tomorrow night or the night after, he should see Donald. The boy was on his guard, of course. It would take awhile.

The prospect of letting this thing drag out into the middle of the week was less pleasant than getting it over with right away. At least he didn't have to play cagey with Donald. Steeling himself for anything, he dialed the Millardson number.

Donald said, sure he'd like to spend the evening with him. But he had another engagement. "Why don't you spend that time with Robin? She's far nicer company than I am. So clean. So pure." His voice seemed to lick over the idea. "And let us be honest, Mr. Spokane. You can't stand the sight of me let alone an entire evening together. But you did respond to my little sister. I really think you should entertain her tonight. In my absence. It will be perfectly harmless, I assure you."

Eric's first impulse was to hang up. "You're on my list, Donald. Not your sister. If you can't make it tonight, how about tomorrow?"

"Unfortunately, I'm busy tomorrow also. I'm afraid you'll have to play the game my way, if you want me to play with you at all, Mr. Spokane. Now, I'll call Robin and you can invite her out . . . or whatever you wish."

As Eric waited for Robin to come to the phone, he tried to piece together Donald's motives. It didn't seem plausible that he would be anxious to have his sister go out with men. If anything, Donald should want to keep her secluded. If she fell in love with someone, if she married and moved out of the house, that would take Robin away from him.

"Hello, Eric. Donald tells me you wanted to see us tonight."

That she could sound so open, so unaware of what was going on around her, amazed him for the second time. "Yes. I was hoping we could be with each other under less formal circumstances, if you're willing." He half hoped that she would decline. Using Robin as bait for her brother made him feel lousy rotten.

"I would like to. Except that Donald's busy. Will you see me alone? I seem to be moping around today. You could pull me out of it, if you wanted to spend the time."

She didn't sound mopey at all. "That would be time well spent," he said.

"Six o'clock will be fine, then. And as you say, nothing formal."

"Right."

He hung up the receiver, not knowing whether he hated Donald or himself more for doing this.

At the same time he was curious about Robin. He couldn't deny that he was looking forward to an interesting evening. He might even learn something about Donald through her.

Anticipating how she would dress, he put on a sports shirt and zelan jacket, zipping it halfway closed and turning up the collar. The five o'clock shadow gave his face a certain hardness but he wasn't out to play Little Lord Fauntleroy with her. And if he had judged Robin correctly, she wouldn't give a damn how he looked.

When he came up the block, he saw Robin standing in front of the house, talking to an old lady with a poodle. He had been right about her appearance. Dressed in camel colored slacks and the famous sandals, she looked at this distance like a high school kid, her cropped head fragile in profile, yet animated with sturdy life.

She spotted him, nodded goodbye to the woman and came to meet him half way along the block. An undercurrent of questions was challenging him. That she would consent to meet him at all on such short notice and that she had not waited for him to call for her at the apartment were not the characteristic behavior expected of a wealthy girl. This freedom from artificiality pleased him. At least it would please him if he could be sure that it was her own idea and not Donald's.

"It's going to be a beautiful night," she said, getting into step with him. "I wish we were high up someplace, where we could look out across the horizon."

But he was looking at her, appreciating her own natural bloom of color. She was enough horizon for any man, her hair burnished copper in the growing twilight.

"I'll settle for a coffee house, though," she smiled. "Why don't you take me to the Village, Eric?" She linked her arm through his as they crossed Fifth Avenue. "We can ride the bus all the way down town. I remember years ago when I was a baby, Dad used to take me on the double deckers. They were fun."

"Why not?" But he wasn't pleased to take her there. He didn't like the idea of sitting this young girl in the middle of Bohemia. Something in him wanted to keep her in a glass cage where nothing of human dirt and misery could touch her.

They waited with a group of others for the Washington Square bus. The evening breeze played with her hair. He wanted to touch it and feel the silky texture.

"I'm glad you want to be our friend," she said out of nowhere.

"You must have plenty of friends." The bus pulled up and they were caught in the crowd to the door, preventing her from answering him right then.

They moved to the back but there were no vacant seats. She caught the hanger and they swayed together as the bus swayed through the traffic. People jostled them. Children going home from Central Park zoo floated their balloons between them. He wanted her to keep on talking but she couldn't now. The idea of a coffee house seemed suddenly right. There they could have the required privacy and all the unmolested time in the world for each to say whatever was necessary. She did not make him feel like a stranger. An area of warmth moved out from Robin to touch him. They might have known each other for years, he felt today. The natural reserve which she had shown in front of her family had softened. And she did not move away with annoyance when the bus bumped them together. Instead, she laughed, as though she knew he could not have meant to take advantage of the crowded situation. He felt that she trusted him, as people do sometimes, instinctively. And he intended to prove to her that this trust was well placed.

They got out and strolled down Eighth Street where men in dungarees and beards mingled with women in their mink stoles. He saw a young boy clad in walking shorts go over Robin's body with his eyes, then stare hard at himself digging to see what was happening. The challenge jolted him, as he realized he was steering Robin through the crowds, holding her lightly by the elbow as though she were already in his possession.

They talked little as they walked, each content just to be here and together for the moment. He refused to think about the difference tomorrow would bring for them both. Class consciousness was out of style. Yet he had to face the fact that he wouldn't be here with Robin if he weren't in her father's employ. The impulse to square with her bulged up into his throat. Yet he could not tell her about Donald.

They turned down at MacDougal Street and found a coffee shop less crowded than most. An ornate place with heavy wooden tables and chairs upholstered in red plush. She went directly to one of the alcoves that looked out on the street and leaned back into the nook of the wall.

He extended a menu toward her, but she shook her head.

"I always take cappuchino," she said.

"Oh? I didn't realize that you came here that often."

"I don't. Anymore."

The waiter appeared and bowed over them.

"Two cappuchinos," Eric said. He took out a pack of cigarettes and put it on the small round table.

Couples strolling on the street peered in, holding their glances on Robin for as long as they could.

"You have an audience," he said.

"Do I? I was watching that bar across the street. The soldiers and sailors who go in. Most of them come out alone. It must be very lonely in a strange city with no one to call." Her own voice echoed their loneliness. Instantly she turned it off. "See, I am mopey today. Donald was right."

"Mope away then." He did not want to force her to speak. Better to let the feeling trickle out of her naturally. But he could not really let the subject drop. He felt a need to get beneath the gentle exterior, to hear the sound of the deep waters running there. "I can feel sorry for the sailors. But how am I expected to feel sorry for you? It would be hard to believe that you don't have friends."

As he said the words, he realized that it wouldn't really be hard to believe at all. Donald was enough to scare away anyone. Yet it was Donald who had encouraged this friendship. He wondered if Donald's behavior was restricted to himself in this instance.

She had taken the match book and lighted the candle on the table. It glowed in front of her face as she gazed into the pear-shaped flame. The scrutiny of its brightness revealed the unblemished texture of her skin. Then she cupped her hands around the light, almost reading his thoughts. The outline of her lips in flickering shadow was the outline of sadness, though the corners tilted upward. He wanted to take her hand or tuck a coverlet over her knees against the chillness of ghosts that seemed to be floating in her silentness.

"Yes, I do have friends," she said.

"You could sound a little more enthusiastic." He spoke gently, wanting her to know that he was on her side, not chiding her or being flip.

The waiter came, placing their cups and folding napkins beside the spoons.

She lifted her spoon and began to stir it through the fluffly white cream, moving the scatter of cinnamon down into the liquid. "Let's not talk about me all night," she said briskly, recovering from the thoughts which had enveloped her. "Let's talk about you. After all, I don't know anything at all about you yet. And I'd like to."

He wanted to ask her why. Why should she want to know about an ordinary guy stuck away in an office five days a week. "All right," he said. "Shall I begin with my love life or the wild jungle escapade in Africa when I was surrounded by six elephants and three tigers."

"Tell me about the tigers, Eric."

The way she said his name always made him pause. She gave life to the word, the syllables became straight and dignified. "Well, this is how it is with tigers. They have a very unpredictable nature." And he found that he was telling her all about Cee-Zee.

From the way she listened, he knew she understood he was talking about a woman. The subject didn't offend her. On the contrary, she listened with an interest that flattered him.

"And you," he concluded. "Have you hunted tigers too?"

She grinned and her nose crinkled across the bridge with hearty amusement and knowledge. "All the tigers I've ever known were on a leash. Somebody else's."

He had not taken her for the kind who would allow herself involvements with married men. "Even Cuban tigers?"

"Especially Cuban tigers. And Portuguese tigers. And Italian tigers."

"Have you ever tried the home-grown variety? They come fierce and free, you know."

She looked at him slowly and he had the feeling that she thought him very naive. "For American tigers, one needs a permit."

"Yes, I understand," he said.

"Do you?" She moved a cigarette out of the package and lit it from the candle. Then she rested both elbows on the table and put her chin on the bridge of her clasped hands.

He moved the candle aside so he could look at her and so she could see him clearly. "Supposing I tell you that permits are not as difficult to obtain as you believe."

"I would say, prove it to me."

He drew in a long breath, calculating how far he could go with Robin and still not reveal what he was up to with Donald. "How hard have you tried?"

The smoke curled before her eyes, wending its languid path upward. "Need I tell you?" she said.

"Please do."

She surveyed him for a minute, feeling, testing. "All right," she said at last. "There is first the family tree to consider. The roots of it seem to twist up and tangle themselves into the branches."

"In plain language?"

"In plain language, my great-grandmother and my grandmother and my mother have each produced one child who was not quite acceptable. I don't mean insane, that would be easier to cope with, I think. And each of them, in her turn, has committed suicide. Shall I stop now, Eric?"

"No. Go on, please."

She unclasped her hands and stroked off ash from her cigarette into the milk-glass tray beside her cup. "You should stop me now, you know. It's silly to be frightened by heredity."

"Nothing that frightens one is silly." He cast about for means to reassure her.

"But it is silly, whether one admits it or not." She sipped at her coffee, the words hanging definite between them. "I wouldn't want a son who couldn't adjust himself to living. And who couldn't be helped to adjust. I think I might kill myself too."

"Surely you don't believe that people can't be helped. Especially if therapy is begun at an early age."

"And how do you guarantee that one can spot the symptoms at an early age? Some children play together, exhibit kindness, intelligence, willingness to cooperate, good humor. All the things that one wishes in a child. How do you tell, Eric, that they are doomed to grow up the inheritors of a family weakness that destroys them slowly from the inside? Yes, how do you find this out until it is already too late? Until the child has deteriorated, morally and physically, beyond recuperation?" She spoke with a quiet vehemence, the numb flatness of despair giving a certain dignity to her speech and mellowing the youth in her features.

He sat back, not wanting to answer her right away, not wanting to respond off the top of his head. She had given him the gift of her honesty. He must give her in return the gift of his thoughtfulness.

"I don't know," he said. "But I hope that medical science is a little more adequate now than it was forty years ago, thirty. Even twenty."

"And you would be willing to gamble on that?"

"I am a gambler by nature, Robin."

She lifted a drop of melted wax onto her finger and flattened it with her thumb. "That is because you are not a woman, Eric. There is a mysterious something in the process of carrying a child in one's body and giving it birth. I remember touching my mother's belly when it was high. Feeling the child kick within her. I remember the expression on her face, its mixture of hope and love and fear. Yes, a man can be equally attached to his children. My father's love is as great as any man's. But in our family, it is not the man who must deal with the responsibility. That is the obstacle, you see. The burden of blame more painful than birth itself."

He lifted his cup. The coffee had cooled and he realized they had been sitting there for a long time, though it hardly seemed more than a moment. The sky had lost its light now and a sprinkling of stars shone beyond the reddish glare of the neon lights across the street.

"And so," she concluded, "I find it best to hunt tigers that are leashed."

"You speak as though they can't be as dangerous."

"Well, they can't," she said with conviction.

Eric lifted an eyebrow in silent question.

"I am a coward, you see. I can always skip off to another country without feeling I've cheated."

"Without feeling you have cheated yourself either?"

"I've been through that phase a thousand times. One has to compromise somewhere."

She looked about her at the young couples who had taken various seats around the room. The soft atmosphere lent itself to intimacies out of place uptown. Men felt free to hold the hands of the women across from them.

Eric followed her gaze and then looked back at her. "You don't sound convinced," he said.

"But I have no choice."

He took a breath and said, "Perhaps Donald isn't so badly off as you think? Supposing I could prove it to you?"

She looked at him incredulously. "Sweet Eric," she said with infinite softness. "It's not Donald. You haven't met my other brother. You never shall."

The words left him speechless. Donald was certainly bad enough. If there was something worse than Donald in the family, he didn't want to see it.

"You don't look so sure of yourself now," she said. Her cup was empty and she tilted it to gaze into its bottom.

"I didn't realize," he admitted. "But that doesn't mean I'm ready to give in."

"As you wish. But Donald and I have a pact. We made it long ago and nothing can dissolve it. Yes. We promised each other never to involve a stranger in our lives. Better to let the bad seed die with us."

"And your father, does he know about this?"

She smiled with satisfaction. "Of course not. He couldn't bear the shame. Or the knowledge that eventually all his vast fortunes will go to charity. Yet sometimes I think he suspects and cannot allow himself to believe the truth of his suspicion. I feel sorry for my father. But I would feel sorrier if he lived to see his grandchildren with the other inheritance than his money."

Eric signalled for more cappuchino, needing a breathing spell to organize her revelations to him.

She accepted the second cup, drawing it closer to her and dropping sugar slowly to sift through the cream. "I suppose you are wondering why I'm telling you this when we hardly know each other."

He had flattered himself into believing that Robin considered him a friend. "Yes," he said slowly.

"Because I want you not to urge Donald into something that would destroy our promise."

Eric took a cigarette now and struck a match just to hear the sound and to watch the sulfur flare. "Then you know."

"Yes, of course. Dad has gone through this a dozen times. So far he has been unsuccessful."

"Then why do you lose confidence now?"

Robin pulled her jacket close as though protecting herself from a sudden threatening coldness. "Simply intuition," she said. Her eyes were luminous oceans bright and silvery as though a new moon were shining behind them.

Eric signalled for the check, then reached across and put his hand over hers. "You're right to respect that intuition," he said kindly. "I would like to know that you aren't afraid of it."

She looked at him, her lips parted just a little. He knew that she was afraid. Afraid for Donald. And certainly afraid for herself.

CHAPTER EIGHT

Monday morning as he dressed for the office, Eric was still thinking about her. He went out and got toast and coffee at one of the local hamburger joints, too engrossed with the problem of Robin to bother fixing his own breakfast. The new knowledge of why Donald was unwilling to be fixed up with a woman began to alter his plans. The toast tasted dry and rough in his mouth. All of him felt rough and his impulse was to tell Millardson the deal was off. If he had any sense, he would get out from under. He didn't want to be the focal point of so many lives. And he could feel his freedom slipping away again, as a result. No use kidding himself. Stupid or not, he had to go through with this thing.

He rode upstairs in the jammed elevator and strode through the clatter of typewriters to his own cubicle overlooking Madison Square Park. It wasn't much of an office. Papers stacked on his battered desk. More papers piled on top of the scratched cabinets. The Millardson account could move him upstairs, give him an air-conditioned office and a private secretary. But the money alone wasn't enough reason. He knew he would be just as glad to get the hell out of here altogether and start bumming around again. Except there was more to it than the money. Robin's future was a precious commodity to him in a way he couldn't explain. He picked up one of the ball point pens and began scribbling policy sheets, letting the back of his mind work out what was to be done concerning Donald.

When the lunch break arrived, he decided to collect the favor Cee-Zee owed him.

He ducked out of the office and headed for a private phone booth, hoping it was still early enough to get Geraldine in.

The phone rang seven times and he was about to hang up when her voice answered, out of breath.

"I was halfway down the steps already," she said with annoyance. "What d'you want?"

He knew he was taking a chance. Geraldine was hardly someone to count on. She had no reason to be on his side rather than Lilio's. Regardless of whether Lilio found out or not, he said, "Will you tell Cee-Zee to call me? Will you do that, Geraldine?"

"Is this the big dough you promised me?"

"When Cee-Zee calls, I'll send you twenty as a starter."

"Chicken feed. You're a phoney, mister, and I got no time to play."

"If she's a friend of yours, you'll tell her to call whether you like me or not."

"Sure. And get the boss breathing down my neck. Not on your life."

"All right then. Can you tell me where I can reach her?"

"I don't know nothing."

The receiver slammed in his ear.

He sat for awhile in the stifling phone booth adjusting himself to the fact that the only way he could contact Cee-Zee would be by going to get her. This meant running into Lilio again.

The rest of the afternoon he fiddled away restlessly, watching the hands of the big clock at the other end of the room. His patience ebbed low. But beyond that, he felt the security that Cee-Zee wouldn't let him down.

He was cold sober and steady when he reached Lilio's joint. A heavy gray fog rolled in from the Hudson, blanketing the houses and smudging the street. The long searching voice of a boat horn stretched up from the water. Reality seemed a million miles away. He took the steps to the door on one jump and pushed his way inside.

The place was not as crowded tonight. He spotted Geraldine standing idly at the back wall, looking ridiculous in her gauzy apron. The few customers were apparently steadies, most of them dull from too much alcohol and unable to take other advantage of the service than to call an occasional obscenity after the disappearing behinds of the girls who served their drinks.

He had no sane reason to think that Cee-Zee would be here tonight but it was his only chance of contact. Working his way past the tables, he approached Geraldine. She looked at him without enthusiasm and pretended to busy herself behind the bar.

"Hi," he said and dropped a five spot on the counter. "Remember me?"

She glanced at the money and shrugged. "Never saw you before. Why don't you go home?"

"I'll go home." He added another five. "Soon. Now be a nice girl and save us all a lot of trouble."

She uncorked a fresh bottle of Scotch and poured half of it into another bottle partially filled with water, then screwed on a shot measure. The sheen of her white hair curved in a stiff wig-like page boy around her shoulders.

"Come on, be nice," he coaxed, adding another bill to the pile. "Business is lousy tonight anyway."

She surveyed the fifteen dollars and stroked her cheek.

"Money is a girl's best friend, isn't it?" He climbed up on the bar stool and waited.

"Nobody's here," she said, taking the money. "I don't know where your girl friend is. She doesn't tell me her secrets."

He grabbed her hand and squeezed the wrist. "Quit stalling me, girl. I'm in no mood."

"You're hurting my arm," she whined, her face screwing up.

"It'll get worse if you don't talk."

"Well, where do you think she is, stupid?" Her head motioned to the back room.

He had the sickening feeling that he would walk inside and find Cee-Zee with the chimp. And there wasn't much he could do about getting her out of there in a rush if she were undressed.

A man's raincoat hung over the back of a chair. He grabbed it up, then ducked in through the little door to the back room.

She was undressed all right, practically naked in black bra and panties. She stood in high heels on top of an upright piano, belting out, "Some of these days, you're gonna miss me, honey" in a raucous voice that barely carried the tune. She held a lifesized rag doll in one arm and bumped her belly against it at the end of each line of song. Her eyes were closed and her body wavered, threatening to tumble off the piano at any moment. The half a dozen people in the dimness were singing along with her. Lilio stood in the shadows, chewing a long thin cigar, nodding and chuckling to himself. There was nobody at the piano.

He had to do it fast. Taking three steps to the piano, he jumped up on the stool and grabbed Cee-Zee. He pulled her down. Her knees buckled under her drunken weight. He held her up by the waist and tossed the coat over her.

"You're a dead man, monsieur," Lilio's voice rang out.

Instinctively Eric ducked at the words, letting Cee-Zee fold up with him. A knife whizzed past his shoulder and landed with a whanging sound in the piano. He started to drag Cee-Zee toward the door. The audience sat dumbfounded, not knowing whether or not this was part of the act. Lilio made it to the door in a few bouncing movements. Bracing Cee-Zee in one arm, Eric smashed his fist into the soft face. He felt the mushy mashing of bones beneath the fat. The force of his blow spun Lilio half around. A woman screamed. He brought his knee up into Lilio's groin. The man jackknifed and tumbled to the floor.

Eric didn't want to watch. He kicked the door open, pulling Cee-Zee outside, across the length of the room. They banged into tables, knocking over bottles and glasses. The crashing, shattering sound of glassware made a noisy path toward the exit.

They came out into the fog. He tried to stand her on her own feet. Stumbling and tripping, she hung onto his collar. He had to hold the raincoat closed as it flapped open to reveal her scanty underthings.

He made it with her to Broadway and searched through the weather for the lights of a taxi, glancing back every so often to see that no one had come out after them.

A cab finally pulled up and he shoved Cee-Zee inside and climbed in beside her, telling the cabbie his address. She crumpled up in a corner of the seat. He came close to her and slapped her cheeks lightly, realizing that she didn't smell of liquor. He lifted an eyelid and saw that the iris had rolled up toward the top of her head. He moved a hand inside the raincoat and felt beneath her warm breast for the beating of her heart. The rapid thudding did not reassure him. For all he knew, he had a potential corpse beside him.

"You better make it to the hospital," he called to the cabbie. "And quick."

For what seemed like hours, he paced the corridor. The sound of his own shoes clicked loudly in his ears. He felt for cigarettes and found the package empty. He crumpled it and flung it into an urn of sand. A white clad nurse glided by. She smiled at him and he scowled back. He jammed his hands into his pockets and went down the antiseptic smelling hall to the desk attendant bending over a magazine in the yellow arc of lamplight.

"Where can I get cigarettes in this place?" His nerves were too knotted to bother with politeness.

'You can't," she said blandly. Then she opened a desk drawer. "But please take these. We keep them for emergencies."

"Thanks." He dropped a fifty cent piece on the blotter and went back to his vigil outside the emergency ward.

His shirt felt bathed with sweat. He sat down on a wooden bench, leaning his head back against the unyielding wall.

An intern finally came out. Patches of skin showed through his close shaven head. "Miss Walter will be all right," he said. "But I'm afraid there are a few complications."

Eric stood up. "What kind? What do you mean?" He felt sopped through with nicotine but he lit another cigarette anyway.

"I mean legal ones. Miss Walter is suffering from an overdose of delauded hydrochloride. Narcotics. I'm sorry, but we'll have to notify the police."

Eric let the smoke out in a long silent breath. A chill prickled up along his neck. Cee-Zee wasn't a dope addict. He knew that. It didn't make sense to him. She had too much on the ball to go after this kind of kicks.

"Can I see her?"

"Are you a relative?"

"Yes."

"She's in no condition to speak with anyone but if you want to go in for a few minutes…"

"Thanks."

He pushed through the swinging doors and found her yellow white and sweating. Carefully he took one clammy hand into his own.

"Honey, it's me, Eric. Can you speak? What happened?"

She swallowed hard and tried to open her lips. They were cracked and dry. "I'm thirsty… nauseous."

A nurse came up with a pan and put it beneath Cee-Zee's chin. Her body heaved with tearing wrenches but nothing came up except a thin stream of saliva. Eric held the pan and motioned the nurse away.

"She can't have anything to drink. I'm sorry," the nurse said.

"Everyone's so sorry around here," he muttered. Then, turning to Cee-Zee, he said, "Can you tell me what happened, kid? You're in bad trouble."

"I don't know," she said between convulsions.

He sighed, believing her. "Maybe Lilio gave you something. Can you remember?"

"I feel lousy."

"I know. But try to think. You've got to tell me something if we're going to get you out of this."

"Can't think. Nauseous. It hurts. All of me hurts so."

The intern came back. "You'll have to step outside now, Mr. Spokane."

He touched Cee-Zee's forehead with his lips. "Just take it easy and don't worry. I'll see what I can do about getting a lawyer."

Her lips made the effort to smile but her eyes remained smeared with the pain.

"I'll be back in the morning."

He walked through the condensed wetness on York Avenue, trying to figure it. The main thing was that he had to clear Cee-Zee. He felt convinced that it wasn't her fault. A good lawyer, one with lots of drag, could fix it up for her in a hurry.

He sat it out through the rest of the night. At nine A.M. he phoned Millardson.

CHAPTER NINE

The next week became a hectic series of fanagling, the details of which he would never know completely. What galled him most was that Cee-Zee wasn't willing to implicate Lilio. He tried to show her that it would be best for her if Lilio were stashed behind bars for a couple of years. But Cee-Zee remained stubborn. She had her reasons, apparently. And he couldn't pry them loose from her.

Now she was back in his apartment, thinner than usual, not quite so perky. The ordeal had drained her vitality and though the days were getting warmer, she kept herself wrapped in a blanket. He made her drink broth and eat soft boiled eggs. She didn't tell him she was grateful, but she didn't have to. They seemed to have a way of speaking to each other without words. And he knew she wouldn't forget he had saved her, not only from a jail sentence, but her life as well.

He sat opposite her and surveyed this subdued, frail creature, thinking that she was in no condition to help him out with Donald.

"You're looking pretty glum for a hero," she said, mustering fragments of energy. "Because I'm staying here to pull the odd pieces together, you don't have to hold my hand. Why don't you go out and wrestle with that broad who keeps phoning? I'm tired of telling her you're not in."

Eric turned uncomfortably in his chair. "She called again today?"

"Didn't you expect it? She's got a real thing for you." She smiled wryly. "I feel sorry for her."

So do I, Eric thought.

He felt peculiarly helpless about Hilda. The tortures that must be burning up her brain every time she heard Cee-Zee's voice instead of his own were terrible to consider.

"If you ignore her long enough," Cee-Zee said, "she'll do something desperate."

"Maybe she'll go away."

"Not a chance. Some of us aren't built for defeat. And she takes herself very seriously, poor thing. Do me a favor and see her, will you? I think you've got enough troubles as it is."

A band of stubbornness gripped him. Hilda was not going to strong arm him into seeing her. "Let's not talk about it anymore. Let's talk about you, instead."

Cee-Zee laughed aloud with a spark of the old self. "And what exactly is there to say about me? I don't even have the strength to spread my legs."

This was true and he knew it. But he had faith in Cee-Zee's power of recuperation. She wasn't the hypochondriac type. In a couple more days, she'd bounce back on her feet again, the incident with Lilio forgotten, her old, trouble-making self raring for action.

"While you're languishing on your sick bed, let me plant a few seeds in that crazy subconscious of yours."

"That's right," she said shrewdly, "you never did tell me what brought you around in the first place. I don't suppose you wanted to catch my act." There was no malice in her voice. Only humor and the need to be entertained.

He took the bowl of soup from her lap and refilled it from the potful simmering on the stove. The strong chicken odor touched off his own appetite, but not for soup. Six days he'd been living like an invalid to keep Cee-Zee company, the animal strengths lying dormant within him. But now he strained for something more. A juicy steak in one of the better restaurants and a juicy girl afterwards. His nerves were becoming touchy.

Returning with the soup, he spread a fresh napkin on her lap, feeling the roundness of her thighs beneath the blanket. His mind brought up images that took effort to thrust away. The curling triangle between her legs and the oval of her belly button.

"You look like you're suffering, Spooky. I'm sorry I'm such a drag."

"Forget it," he said roughly. "Now, what were we saying?"

"You were going to tell me..."

"Yes, I remember. What brought me into that hell hole." He sat down on the couch and crossed his ankles on the arm. "To tell you the truth, I was out to get a favor from you. A very big favor."

"Don't sound so sad, honey. You're in a terrific position to ask for it now. Ask away."

He hesitated, brushing bits of tobacco from his trousers. Newspapers lay scattered in sections beneath the table. A layer of soot sprinkled on the windowsill, unwashed these many weeks. It occurred to him that the place was really falling apart. He had come a long way since Cee-Zee first walked in the door. A long way down. It was time to bounce up again, higher than he had been before. Push toward progress and all that kind of jazz.

"All right, I'll tell you," he said, sitting up. "There's a certain guy, a real creep of a character, who's worth a good couple of grand to me if I can get him in bed with a woman."

"What's so difficult? Unless somebody cut it off."

"No. He's all man. But for reasons best left unsaid, he is determined never to."

"A swish?"

"Not that either."

Cee-Zee let the spoon drop into her soup. "Well, either you tell me or you don't. What's all this playing footsie if I'm supposed to help?"

"You're right."

He cast about for a way of telling her without implicating Robin. The girl trusted him not to give away the family secret and he had no desire to betray her.

"The guy is afraid of knocking some broad up. I'm positive he won't rely on the usual means of prevention. My guess is that he probably has been fooling around in ways that frustrate him worse than not bothering at all. Voyeurism. Looking at dirty movies. Maybe milk bottles for all I know." And he wanted to add: and he's got a rise for his sister.

"Not another word," Cee-Zee said, leaning over to set the bowl on the rug. "I know what's going through your mind, you bastard." She grinned slyly. "You have a proper respect for my ability to con men into such things."

Eric grinned.

"All I want to know is, what's all this got to do with you? I didn't figure you for the vicarious type."

"I told you. Money. Enough cash to stuff this whole apartment." He moved his arm in a grand gesture.

"You know something?"

"What?"

Cee-Zee pushed away his offer of a cigarette. "I don't believe you."

She said it with a conviction that made him go into a slow burn. He felt as though she had caught him at a banquet with his fly open. "Don't you know that I'm greedy for the bucks?" His voice didn't come out as convincing as he would have liked.

"You should see the color of your face," Cee-Zee laughed. "Try me again tomorrow."

How would it strike her, he wondered, if she knew he was going all out for a girl he didn't have the remotest idea of chasing into bed? The thought made him ashamed of himself. Sissy. Better to keep it to himself than have Cee-Zee scream laughing at him.

"Fine, fine," he said impatiently. "We'll drop it."

"Not so hasty. I didn't say I wouldn't. I just wanted to tickle my idle curiosity. But I guess you'd rather be tickling something else. Anyway, I'm not one to turn my back on a pal. What's a little snatch between friends?" She drew the blanket up to her neck. "If you can give me some time to get in working order again, I'll be glad to put it at your service. For personal use or otherwise."

Eric nodded, thinking that this was a switch for her. He was surprised that Cee-Zee could admit to being grateful. This time, her nonchalance was tempered with something of an almost human heart. He felt a sting of gratification, of progress. He had not lost the game to Cee-Zee yet. The possibility of undermining her independence still existed. This gave him a feeling of exhilaration and he thought it a damn crime to have to waste her on Donald. But one man more or less wouldn't make any real difference to Cee-Zee.

"So get the balls rolling," she said and winked. "I won't even ask for a commission."

He didn't want to think what kind of antics Donald would put her through. He had known many a high priced whore in his day. They really worked to earn their money. He'd seen beautiful women with their behinds bleeding. He'd seen jaws locked in muscle cramp from six hours of steady manipulating. It was a tough thing to ask of Cee-Zee. Yet he knew that she knew the score. This wasn't like leading an innocent lamb to the slaughter.

"When you're on your feet again," he said, "we'll arrange a little party."

"Maybe I should stay on my back," she said with amusement.

In the meantime, he'd better keep in touch with the Millardson clan, Eric thought. He felt nervous about Robin. That she had gone these many years unharmed didn't impress him. And during the time Millardson had been fixing things for Cee-Zee, he had tried not to see Robin at all. Now he had a reason to take her out again.

The raw nerves in his body were creeping up now to muddle his thinking. He wasn't quite sure that he wanted to see Robin so platonically. The demands of his body were too subtle and more intelligent about obtaining their desires than his rational brain. Yes, he wanted to see Robin just to talk to her. But he also felt an anticipation that kindled other feelings. He had never permitted himself to think how she would look undressed. How she would respond to hands groping and fondling the forbidden areas of her body.

He gazed at Cee-Zee, wishing he could take it out on her. But it would be no fun for either of them in her condition.

"You're a mess, Spooky," she said out of nowhere.

"I need to stretch my legs," he said. "I'm going for a walk. Want me to bring you anything?"

"Please," she said, waving her hand at him impatiently, "go already."

He grinned and left her. The driving force in the pit of his stomach moved him around the city without direction. The thought of calling Robin burned bright and compelling in his brain. The coincidence of his physical needs and her pure beautiful body made him distrust himself. He wasn't the kind of man to kibitz with a girl. Nor was he accustomed to being interested in someone who didn't have experience. He began to conjecture just how far she had ever let herself go with the married men she'd known. The thought of frustration hovering behind that innocent face piqued him. If it weren't for that crazy idea in her head, he knew he could show her a good time. No doubt she needed it by now. The notion of women remaining untouched until their wedding night made him laugh sourly. Any normal, full-blooded girl should have sex and plenty of it. Make 'em more normal. The more he thought about her, the more he convinced himself that it would be just as important to work on Robin as on her brother. They both needed the works. And needed it bad.

He stepped into a drugstore and dropped a dime into the slot, dialling the Millardson number before his good sense stopped him.

She consented to see him, without acting coy, without playing hard to get. He felt a pang of guilt that she agreed so readily to meeting him in the Village. Of course she couldn't suspect what lurked behind the casual invitation.

He fidgeted around the half hour, knowing she wouldn't agree to a hotel room. He couldn't take her home. Cee-Zee wouldn't mind. But there were few people as broadminded as Cee-Zee. He strolled around Washington Square circle inspecting the girls and telling himself that he'd have been better off to pick up one of these than start up with Robin.

The honk of a horn caught his attention. He saw that she had pulled up to the curb in a gray Jaguar roadster. The long graceful line of the fenders blended well with her own erect posture. She sat easily behind the wheel with that familiar open smile which suspected nothing.

"Nice little buggy," he said appreciatively.

The red leather seat against her orange striped blouse made a vital combination of color that pulsed through him.

"Get in," she said. "I like to drive."

He got in and pulled the door shut. The resounding clunk gave him a thrill. He stretched his legs out and inhaled the fine odor of the rich leather appreciatively.

She wheeled the car around and they zoomed up Fifth Avenue, the wind flapping the points of her collar against her soft cheek. He leaned against the door and watched her, trying to find her mood. She held the wheel lightly with one hand, resting her other arm on the doortop. He found nothing tense about her that matched his own tenseness. She drove fast because she enjoyed the beautiful machine at her control. He felt like a slavering wolf sneaking down to the chicken yard.

They rode all the way uptown to the George Washington bridge. He didn't mind that she wasn't talking much. In the rush of wind it was hard to speak beneath a shout. They moved across the bridge and she turned for a moment to watch the lights, strung like beads along the highway below.

When they reached the Jersey shore, she made the car climb up the palisades and it moved like a prancing horse, the powerful engine roaring in a low-throated key. They could gallop to Mars, he thought, the stars looked so near.

She parked in the darkness and leaned her arms on the wheel with a sigh. "It's good to be away," she said.

He crossed his legs and kept himself as far away from her as he could in the intimacy of the car. "Away from what?" he said.

"Oh, everything. You like to get away yourself, Eric. Don't try to deny it."

The green smell of country made a bower of fragrance around them. His senses felt enlarged. He wanted to touch and smell and have everything there was to have in the world. Then he remembered he spent forty hours a week locked away from this world. And the most he could ever get out of it was a bankroll not quite large enough to buy him everything he really wanted. He was clawing up the sides of a well that had no top. It made him hungry and restless. For two bits, he would reach out and take this girl. Ignore her silly excuses, forget tomorrow and all the dull tomorrows lapping in endless waves on the dry sand of his lonely beach.

"Sure I like to get away," he said gruffly. He watched fireflies punctuate the darkness. "That's why I called you."

"Yes, I know."

He turned to her now. "Just what do you know, little girl? Tell me."

She opened the door and let it swing. "I know that you're a lonely man looking to take his mind off himself. Just like me, just like my father." She brought one foot up onto the bucket seat and hugged her knees close. "Just like everyone. I hope I can help you a little, Eric."

That was a laugh, Robin helping him. But he couldn't really laugh because it was true in a way. "All right," he said. "Then help me." He touched her elbow lightly and saw his fingers close around her arm.

She studied his grip on her. "I suppose I asked for it, taking you up here like this. But I'm asking you not to ... please." She didn't sound at all frightened. Her voice was matter of fact. She might have been saying, please pass the butter.

"Why not?" The warmth beneath his skin seemed to singe the ends of his nerves. "What have I got to lose? Or you, for that matter?"

"We went through all this, Eric. I thought you understood me."

"I understood. But, you remember, I didn't agree with you."

She sat very still, not struggling with him, paying no attention to the hold he had on her. "But I have a right to think for myself," she said. "Isn't that so?"

He didn't want her to be thinking now. He wasn't thinking, only feeling the pull of her, sensing the flow and sweep of her youth, imagining the rough grunts that would tear from her as they lay on the grass together. That was better than any thinking. Superior to all logic and plans. If he could feel her nipples grow hard between his lips, the insides of her legs quiver and tighten around him. If he could have her yield to the cravings of her own flesh, this was all the thinking he wanted or needed tonight.

"Must you think all the time?" he said.

"I guess we don't really understand each other, Eric. I'm disappointed."

Her straightforward judgment made him release his grip on her arm. "I hope you're spared the regret, the looking back on nights like this one. You probably have lots of them tucked away already. Tell me, Robin, how many times have you brought a man to the end of the road and put up a no-trespassing sign in his face?" He stared out to the necklace of bridge silhouetted against the hazy sky.

"You talk as though I enjoy it. That I do it purposely for the sake of some cowardly amusement." She took a bandana from the glove compartment and tied it around her neck, tucking the ends into the v of her blouse.

"Think about that sometime," he said. "Maybe it's exactly what you do. According to what you've told me, there's never going to be any real sex in your life. Unless you have your tubes tied and make yourself a female eunuch." Frustration was making him coarser than he'd intended. But it was right not to coddle her. "You've got to get your kicks some way. This is as good a start as any. And who knows? Maybe sweet little Donald will introduce you to other more gratifying aspects of perversion. There's a lot been done in that field. Ask him some time."

She put her head back against the cushioned edge of the seat and stared up at the sky. "Thank you for your kindness," she said softly.

"Oh baby, face the facts. Is it kindness you want or realities? What are you, a fifty year old bag with her life behind her? You don't have to conduct yourself as though every time you look at a man, an infant monster'll sprout from between your legs. There are plenty of people with lousy chromosomes who don't lie down in the middle of the floor and die. Maybe I'm being cruel and unsympathetic. The narrow-minded male point of view." He flicked a lock of hair back from his forehead. "But somebody has to challenge this melodramatic approach of yours. And one day some lucky guy'll convince you and won't you be glad."

He felt all talked out. "Now let's go back."

They drove into Manhattan with a different kind of silence between them. He glared at the passing traffic, disgusted with himself for giving Robin the credit of good sense. He felt stony and far removed from her. She was the spoiled kid with too many toys, though he hadn't wanted to recognize it.

He felt lousy but he didn't want to go home at eleven o'clock.

They pulled off the highway at seventy-ninth street. "Are we still speaking?" she said as they waited for a red light.

"Sure," he said between his teeth.

"Then why don't you move closer instead of hanging half way out of the car?"

He was surprised that she wasn't hostile. "I thought you'd want to kick me out," he said.

"Why should I? I believe in the right to personal opinions. And frankly you didn't change my personal opinion of you either. I knew you wouldn't do anything that I didn't want. So far as I'm concerned, we're still friends."

"Fair enough," he said. But he wasn't going to spring back into the jolly companion she wanted. Definitely he had made up his mind that Robin should see things his way. Whether she went to bed with him or not didn't matter, so long as she would agree to go to bed with someone... all the way.

At the same time, he had his own problems. They centered in his groin. He had no intention of going home to spend an uncomfortable night feeling Cee-Zee within arm's reach and knowing he couldn't touch her.

"If we're still friends," he said, "you can do something for me."

"Of course."

"Let me borrow your car tonight. And see me tomorrow."

She grinned easily. "Yes to both questions."

He jammed his foot down on the accelerator and let the Jag carry him. Knifing through the deserted streets released some of his pent up force. He felt himself part of the car's power. He seemed almost to lift off the earth and he kept the speed steady at sixty five, not giving a damn if the cops got on his tail. He turned off at Forty Second Street and slowed for the tunnel. Only vaguely was he thinking of Hilda as a person. She became more of an object, a willing receptacle into which he could release himself. The thought of her spread before him as the universe spread above, and his desire became a sleek rocket moving open throttle toward her.

The sound of the roadster announced his presence in the sleeping town. As he parked in front of the old Buick, he saw a light go on in her upstairs window. She opened the door as he reached it.

He pushed her back into the hallway and planted his mouth on hers, not wanting her to speak, not caring what she had to say. For an instant she struggled, pushing at his shoulders weakly. Then her resistance dissolved. Her arms tightened around his neck, her belly strained against him. She wore a nightgown and all he had to do was lift it up. Her heaving breasts felt overwarm. All of her body seemed to be burning up. Her hands moved quickly over him, her fingers licking at his flesh like shreds of flame.

He pulled her to the dining room table and lifted her onto it, the lace cloth bunching beneath her thighs. The light threw her shadow long and grotesque on the floor and perpendicularly on the wall. Whenever she tried to say something, he closed the words off with his mouth or the palm of his hand. Finally he straddled her shoulders.

She was willing, so willing. He felt her knees come up and jab him in the small of his back, egging him on. Her hands hung on to his belt, then dug into the flesh of his waist. The bursting rocket took off and he felt the convulsions of her throat as she swallowed. But he wasn't through with her yet.

They separated for a moment. She turned over onto her belly. The table creaked beneath their combined weight. It was a solid old-fashioned table he'd purchased in an antique store. He laughed silently, thinking that she would have fainted had she known at the time the use to which they would put it.

He lay down on her back, sliding his hands along her ribs to hold her flattened breasts. His stomach folded to the curve of her buttocks and her legs began to spread. She held them rigidly apart and waited. Through the material of his trousers, he could feel all of her, sweaty and eager. For awhile he lay there tantalizing her, then with a swift jamming motion caught her far up and began pounding, slamming all of her against the table. She would be black and blue in the morning. And love it. Now she clutched the edges of the table to keep herself from sliding. The cloth had tangled between them. He pulled it out of the way and heard it tear. The precious lace wedding present from her folks in New England. He flung it away and it landed dangling off the cushion of a chair.

She worked with him, hitting herself hard on the solid wood, not giving a damn, straining herself upward as far as she could go. Her perspiration and his own soaked through his shirt and it stuck to his chest.

"Never stop," she grunted.

He socked her across the cheek and shut her up.

At their peak he had her pinned to the table top, almost cracking her ribs, surely bruising the front of her. He could feel her gasping for breath, choking for air and with gratification both at the same time.

When he finally slid away and stood up in the semilight, he knew he was completely drained. For awhile he walked around, not turning the lamps on, feeling the pleasant lightness in his limbs, a sensation of floating not quite walking. She sat up on the table. The nightgown had long since disappeared in tatters. He saw her rubbing her arms slowly and she cooed to herself. If she'd said one word, he'd have knocked her teeth in. But she didn't. She merely continued to sit on the table, a contented Buddha in the darkness. When he'd gathered all his perceptions, he straightened out his clothes as much as they could be straightened.

Then he slammed out of the house and gunned the motor, mentally scanning his list of restaurants for the possibilities of getting a good steak at three o'clock in the morning.

CHAPTER TEN

When he got home, Cee-Zee lay dozing in the armchair, a half-finished crossword puzzle tucked beside her. In repose her face looked worn out, strained from the hospital ordeal. All the high living had lowered her resistance. She might be in a good humor and try to kid him into believing she could snap back. But he knew better. She needed care. The proper rest. Good food. He hoped she had enough sense to respect these requirements of her body.

Gently he lifted and carried her into the bedroom, setting her down and pulling the covers over her. She sighed in sleep and turned to hug the pillow. He tip-toed back into the living room and switched off the lights, then came back and got into bed himself.

For awhile he lay and listened to her breathing, trying to understand why she insisted on keeping secret what had happened to her with Lilio. He felt impatient with her for protecting him. But he knew it was not her nature to rat on anyone. She had a strange loyalty to all living creatures, good or bad. "Judge not that ye may not be judged..." It was hard to believe that Cee-Zee might have a core of religious sentiment buried deep inside. He wanted to shake her back into reality, make her realize the danger of enemies as well as the value of friends.

His mind wandered back to Robin and how she treated his insistence. Women were alien creatures to him, hoeing their private paths toward incredible destinations. No matter how close he got to them, he did not feel secure that he was a partner to their total being. Each one seemed to hang a small gate that closed him away. Even Hilda, for all her giving, remained a mystery. And there was precious little he could do about understanding any of them.

The alarm went off at seven o'clock. He reached to shut it off before the noise wakened Cee-Zee. He fell back onto the pillow, aware that he had not slept at all and angry with himself because he had to get dressed now to spend another senseless day with insurance policies that bored him silly. He thought about taking the day off and waiting for sleep to come when it would, getting up afterward at his leisure, messing around the house, talking to Cee-Zee, maybe cleaning his camera after all these months of neglect. The prospect felt good to him and he decided not to go to the office for once. He closed his eyes again and smiled languidly. The rich man. The wealthy Mr. Spokane is in private conference today. The bed sheets felt smooth and appealing to his naked body.

Around noon he felt Cee-Zee turn over and yawn. She lay facing him, her cheek snuggled in between the groove of both pillows. She sighed contentedly.

"Still here?" she said, blinking slowly without concern.

"Yep. For the rest of my days."

"That's nice." She examined the nipple of one exposed breast. "You look better today. Have a good time? I didn't hear you come in."

Eric nodded. In a way, it had been a good time. The mixture of Robin with Hilda made a strange brew. "You were dead to the world."

"Must have been. Don't even remember going to bed."

He grinned and touched the tip of her nose with an affectionate finger. "Wonder why not."

"Oh, I see," she laughed with understanding. "You make a fine, gallant nurse. Only I wish you'd do something about that damned telephone."

And as she said it, the phone began to ring. "See what I mean?"

"We'll tear it out," he said mildly as she handed him the receiver.

"Good afternoon, Mr. Spokane." The reedy thin voice could belong to only one person.

"Yes, Donald," Eric said. "What can I do for you?"

"I called to do something for you." His voice sounded tight-lipped beneath the idle manner.

"And what may that be?" Eric said, enjoying himself.

"I'm sending the chauffeur for Robin's automobile. That will save you the trouble of returning it."

"Very good. But why couldn't Robin tell me this herself?"

"She asked me to phone for her. My sister has decided to take one of her vacations. She won't have time to see you anymore, Mr. Spokane. And neither will I."

Eric heard the receiver drop neatly into its cradle. He handed the phone to Cee-Zee, preoccupied with the question of whether Robin was going away of her own free will or not. He began to surmise that maybe she never left because she wanted to go. Her guilty conscience, egged on by Donald and their pact, might be driving her away now. He felt convinced that Donald, upon discovering that his sister was getting friendly with a strange man, reminded her of her obligation. He could even see Donald getting the tickets for her and making sure she got on the plane. This heredity business made a convenient gimmick for Donald to keep his sister from becoming involved with anyone else.

"You look mad," Cee-Zee said.

"I am." He flung himself out of bed and started to pull his clothes on.

"Too bad you didn't rip the phone out before that call," she mused.

But he didn't hear her. His mind whirled with the problem of getting to Robin before she left. Once out of the country, he knew she was lost to him. She must be stopped now. Made to see that Donald was influencing her. Made to face herself instead of running away.

He leaped down the stairs, taking the flights two jumps at a time, dashed into the car and roared up the avenue, tucking his shirttails in as he drove.

He double parked and ran past the doormen who stared after him. It didn't matter that he looked half out of his mind, his hair uncombed, a straggly beard grubby on his chin, no tie, no jacket.

The elevator couldn't move fast enough. He kept his thumb on the buzzer till Kate opened the door. He whizzed past her surprised face and started banging on the line of closed doors, calling Robin's name as he went.

No answer, no sound except Kate's protesting squeals. He rattled knobs and burst into empty rooms till he opened one final door and saw Donald seated at his desk, turning the pages of a small leather volume.

"You look upset, Mr. Spokane," he said, getting up and pulling the silk cord of his dressing gown tighter. "Did you lose something? May I help you?" His smile spread broad and satisfied, showing the pale gums over his teeth.

In that instant Eric knew that Robin had left. But how long ago? And to where? He strode up to Donald and got him by the throat, pressing his thumbs hard against the pointed Adam's apple.

"Talk or you're dead. I don't care if they hang a murder rap on me." He spoke through tight lips, spitting the words into Donald's face, watching it turn yellow, seeing the eyes begin to bulge. He shook him, he kept pressing the spindly throat.

"Too late," Donald choked. He tried to nod that he was willing to speak.

Eric loosened his grip the barest amount, giving him just enough breath to speak. "When? Where?"

"La Guardia. You're too late... Havana."

He dropped Donald and ran out past Kate, still standing there with her hands to her mouth. The elevator door was just closing. He slid inside.

The Jag nosed and found its way from lane to lane as he sped to the airport. Just the barest chance he could catch her before flight time. His hopes were good because on the phone Donald had said that Robin was leaving, not that she *had* left. He judged that he was twenty minutes behind her from the time of the call. Steadily he pressed the gas pedal, working to shave off that twenty minutes. Dodging around cars at eighty five, he trusted to luck that the highway's radar control would not put the cops on him.

Reaching La Guardia, he leaped over the car door and pushed his way through the milling people inside to the waiting room. Loudspeaker voices blared flight arrivals and departures, men checked luggage weights at counters. He nearly knocked over a smiling stewardess as he combed the crowd for sight of Robin. Then he slipped under the chain past the ticket guard and saw a liner lifting slowly from the runway. He stood for an instant watching it rise into the sky, the pocket of frustration spilling over inside him. Suddenly he cursed himself for a jerk and raced back to the car.

He raced the Jag over the connecting highway between La Guardia and International, praying that his own stupidity hadn't fouled him up. He should have realized that Donald was clever enough to tell him only a half truth. He had to believe that Robin was taking a flight to Cuba. That part of it sounded real enough. But he knew damned well Donald had given him the wrong airport.

The same loudspeaker, the same crowds. He shouldered his way through them, boring a swift line of vision above the blonde heads and grays and chestnuts, finding no sign of her, no woman who remotely resembled the brushed auburn cut. Not on the lines, not on the field outside where mechanics tinkered with engines of the huge waiting planes.

Satisfied that she had not stepped into the rest room for a minute, ashamed of himself for having missed her, he jangled the change in his pocket and thought what to do next. Even if he took a flight to Cuba himself, it was a big place to look for one little girl. All he could think of was to go back and finish Donald off. At least then Robin would be free for the next man who became interested.

He dropped silver into a vending machine and watched the cigarettes and matches plop down. Listlessly he pulled off the cellophane and tapped a cigarette against the back of his hand. Then he struck a match and started to lift it toward the tobacco, suddenly dropping them both as he saw Robin walking behind the chauffeur who carried the small valises. His whole world lit up with a brighter flame than any match. Waves of warmth moved over his back. For a few moments, he stood very still, enjoying the satisfaction and the immense security of having succeeded in arriving before she did.

She didn't spot him. She looked blankly ahead of her, puppet-like behind the chauffeur, a sweater dangling carelessly over her arm. This was the first time he had seen her without the semblance of a smile. She seemed bereft of pride, stripped naked so that only her aching heart showed. But she held her head high, looking very much the rich, untouchable heiress. Untouchable. The double meaning of his expression stabbed him into moving toward her now. He did not want to delay the conquering of all the obstacles still looming before Robin could feel free to do with her life as she chose.

"Hello," he said mildly. "I came to return the car."

She looked at him speechless, her dry lips half parted. The chauffeur went to the weighing platform with her luggage.

"I didn't think you would leave without saying goodbye to an old friend," he said, knowing the challenge of his words.

She still hadn't recovered herself. Her eyes had a numb glow to them. He wondered if she heard what he was saying. In the silence he lit another cigarette and gave it to her. "I had a fine chat with your brother," he said. "He doesn't appreciate me at all."

She turned half away from him and managed to find her voice. "I don't think you have a right in my affairs," she said. The words danced on strings which sounded as though Donald pulled them.

"I haven't," Eric said. "Only an interest. A very sincere interest. We haven't known each other very long, Robin, but somehow I can't be convinced that you would go away so abruptly. We had a date this evening, remember."

She couldn't turn to face him. He walked around to face her instead. "What about that date?" he continued.

"You're making this too painful for me," she said, pulling deeply on the cigarette but unable to have it steady her.

"Look," he said, "we don't have to talk about this here. If you really want to go to Cuba, I won't try to stop you. Believe me. I only ask that you give us an hour to talk it over. There's always another plane leaving. Donald doesn't have to know." He resisted an impulse to put his hands on her shoulders to comfort her, to share some of his assurance with her. "What do you say?"

Robin shook her head no. "It's impossible," she said in a barely audible whisper.

"Nothing's that impossible. If you won't do it for yourself, then do it for me."

Her eyes searched his, their green depths dark with question.

"I nearly killed your brother, trying to find out what happened to you. Maybe I would go back and finish the job if it turns out that you're so afraid of him you haven't the freedom to take an hour away from the plans he makes for you to follow. Do you want me to face a prison sentence?" He spoke half jokingly, half serious.

"What did you do to him?"

"Nothing yet. He may have a sore throat for awhile, but it'll clear up."

"You're a coward, Eric."

He took her cigarette and puffed on it. "And you?"

She paused and passed a hand over her tired eyes. "I guess I don't know what I am."

"Then maybe we'd better help you find out."

The chauffeur returned with her baggage stubs and she sent him home.

"I'm getting on the next plane, regardless of what you think you have to say to me, Eric."

He took her arm and led her out to the Jag. "That's a deal," he agreed, watching her squint up at him in the sunshine.

He drove slowly out into Long Island, repeating in detail everything that had happened between himself and Donald. Sensing Robin's amazement, he emphasized the less flattering aspects of her brother's behavior. No doubt she had never permitted herself to see that Donald also was a coward.

For the flight she had put on a sky blue shirtwaist dress. It's skirt billowed in the breeze, reminding him of an ad for Rheingold, as she crossed her legs and let the golden day warm her face.

He brought the car up in front of a roadside restaurant where a few college students sat before french frieds and hamburgers talking about coming finals. He had chosen the place deliberately. The hopeful atmosphere of young people would be better for her than dark corners and the morbid implications of liquor in the middle of the day.

"All we ever seem to do," she said, "is sit someplace and disagree." She tried to smile but most of her was off thinking about other things. He had a tough battle to face with Robin. It occurred to him with sudden clarity that there was nothing in it for him except the dubious satisfaction of being right. He thought back to himself breathing down her neck last night and it handed him a laugh. She was hardly more than a college kid herself. Better educated perhaps, because of the Millardson treasury. But certainly not more mature. A very little girl sat opposite him, filled to brimming with confusion and doubts. Neither romantic nor alluring, these troubles of a little girl. Facing the reality of his position, Eric wondered at the unnamed force compelling his interest in her.

He ordered open steak sandwiches and coffee for them both, taking his time about starting the battle again.

"You're looking for the right words, aren't you?" she said. "I feel sorry, Eric, that you have to go to all this trouble for nothing."

"Thanks for the sympathy." He caught the reflection of himself in the plate glass window, his unkempt head and fierce eyes beneath the heavy ridges of brow. "You know, looking at myself over there," he said, "makes me wonder why Donald thinks I'm such a threat to you."

"He thinks that about every man."

The hint of shyness tinging her words made him examine her. She opened her purse quickly and started to rummage through its contents.

"Do you need something," he said, "or are you managing to avoid me by messing around in that?"

"Of course I'm avoiding you," she said, still unable to look at him. "Because I don't understand why you care what happens to me."

"You know something?" Eric said, shutting the flap of her purse so that she had to look at him. "That makes two of us."

Neither of them jumped to fill in the silence with a quip. Eric handed her the ketchup bottle and the salt. Then she set the bottle near his plate. Someone dropped coins into the juke box. A rock and roll number crooned in four part harmony. They remained serious and quiet, watching each other while they ate. Now that he had stopped fighting with her, Eric felt that she was beginning to give in to him. He was trying to influence her because of a compulsion and not to prove a scientific theory. All his cards lay on the table without a single ace in the hole.

"I don't know what to do about you," she said finally.

"For a start, how about trusting me? We can get you a little place around here. Donald doesn't have to know that you didn't leave the country. Maybe together we can work this thing out. For both our sakes."

Slowly she unwrapped a cube of sugar.

"You don't like the sound of it?" he continued. "You think it's dishonest to do something behind Donald's back?"

"I can go to Cuba for a week. That won't hurt anything."

"And when you come back, it'll start all over again. Sooner or later, you'll have to do something that Donald won't approve."

"Like what?"

"Like living your own life."

The color drained from her cheeks. He had hit home. "Do anything you want, Robin. But believe in it for yourself. I don't think your father is so proud of you for nothing. He says you're a real firecracker."

Now she smiled for the first time that afternoon.

"And I have faith that he isn't mistaken," Eric concluded. "The rest is up to you."

He watched her struggle to distill meaning from her confused emotions. She drank three cups of coffee, clasping and unclasping her fingers. Occasionally she breathed a little sigh.

"I do trust you, Eric. Try to believe that. But I can't go into hiding like a convict. Let me get on that plane. I need to be alone, away from everything and everyone. That'll give me a chance to think. It won't be running away this time. It'll be really thinking."

"And when you return?"

"I'll get in touch with you first. I promise."

He had reached an impasse with her and he knew it. All he could do now was trust her native intelligence and her courage.

"All right," he said. "I'll settle for that."

Mutely, she thanked him.

They drove back to the airport. He waited with her for the plane. They shook hands before she went out onto the field. Then impulsively she reached up and kissed him on the cheek.

He watched her go, saw the easy line of her lithe body mingling with other passengers. She wouldn't turn around to wave to him and he didn't want her to. No goodbyes between them.

CHAPTER ELEVEN

He drove back home figuring what the odds were. He didn't even know who was waiting for Robin in Cuba. Till she got back, the thing was out of his hands.

He found a parking spot across the street from his house, then went to a delicatessen to pick up a few things for Cee-Zee. She was a fiend for cole slaw, he had discovered, so he might as well feed her cole slaw to egg on her lagging appetite. That she wasn't eating too well worried him. She pushed away vitamin pills and she wouldn't eat cereal. Nothing could scare her into taking care of herself. So he bought pastrami and corned beef and a loaf of rye bread just so she would put something into her stomach.

With two heavy bags in either arm, he came into the hall. From the corner of his eye, Eric saw something move. Fists hurtled at his face. Cannon balls seemed to shoot into his chest and belly. The packages fell with a splatter. He started at the three men. Then he felt his head crack open. The men spun in his blurred vision. He sped into total darkness.

When he came to, he was sprawled out, his nose lying in smashed pickles. He got himself into a sitting position and felt his aching head carefully. An egg shaped swelling was growing larger by the second on his scalp. He blinked a few times and wiped his face on his shirt sleeve. Each breath he took made him wince. He got to a standing position, unconsciously taking up one of the small bags which had escaped destruction. Painfully he made his way up the steps and pushed into the apartment.

"Brought you some lunch," he said from between thick lips.

"Mary, Joseph and Jesus!"

"Sh. Softly," he said, flopping into a chair.

He sat with his eyes closed, feeling the lids too soft, too spongy to hold open.

A wet cloth touched over his face. "Hold that," she said softly. "I'll get some ice."

A few moments later, he felt the cold wet pressure of ice against his head.

"Anything broken?" she asked.

"Dunno." He concentrated on trying to breathe around the sticking pain. Gradually it dulled till he could tell that his ribs were still intact.

She got his shirt off and dabbed the cold cloth over the reddening knuckle prints. "You look beautiful," she said. "Just beautiful."

He touched his nose gingerly and sensed the puffiness around his eyes. "A real mess, huh?"

"To put it mildly. Keep your hands away."

Her own warm hands took his away from his face. "Dizzy? Nauseous?"

"Just out of breath."

"I know, hero. We better get you into bed."

"Don' wan' t'move." He spiralled away into darkness again, swaying on black waves.

She pushed his head down between his knees. "Stay like that. I don't go for any fainting around here." Then she got a glass of whiskey and passed it beneath his nostrils.

He grabbed it and swallowed the liquid in one gulp, feeling the stuff begin to brace him.

"Gettin' better … better all the … time."

Now he opened his eyes and the room was sitting in place. "Woosh. Today April Fool's Day or somethin'?"

"If it is, you got corny friends." She was sitting on the arm of the chair half dressed, her hair tied in a roll on the top of her head.

"You look cute anyway." He smiled and felt his face go mushy.

"Well, what did you do to the other guy?" she said hopefully.

"Not a damn thing. I was coming in the house, with lunch for you, sweetie, and bang crash. That's it."

He saw her frown. "Let's get you to sleep for awhile. You can work this out later."

He let her help him to the bed. The soft, comforting mattress embraced him.

The piercing odor of strong coffee awakened him. He wondered what the deuce he was doing in bed this hour of the day. As he turned over, the twisting pain of bruised muscles reminded him. "Hey, in there."

"Stay put," she called back. "I'll bring the coffee into you."

He managed to sit up. The strange head on his shoulders felt large and square and heavy.

Cee-Zee entered carrying a tray with two cups on it. She put the tray on his lap and he lifted one of the cups shakily. The steaming liquid burned his tongue, but it felt good along his insides.

"And now you see how Lilio fights back," she commented, lifting her own cup to her lips.

"What makes you think it's Lilio?"

"Got any other pals?"

"Plenty."

"Oh, I didn't know you were so well liked." She had put on a nylon blouse, leaving the buttons open down the front. A tiny pink rosette stitched to the middle of her brassiere moved with her breathing.

"I'm a doll," he said. "A living, breathing doll."

He continued drinking the coffee, thinking that sure, it could've been Lilio. But it also could've been Donald. He had no real way of deciding. And no matter which of the two had done the job, there still remained the possibility of the other one doing it over again. More thoroughly. He thought of Robin on her way to Cuba and now he was glad that he wouldn't have to see her for a week.

"You know what I think?" Cee-Zee said. "I think it's time for you to take a long vacation. Away from New York. The hell with your job. You can't go into work looking like a hamburger anyway." She spoke uneasily.

"Come on, girl," he said, resting the cup and motioning for a cigarette. "You're not scared, are you?"

She took the tray away and shoved it onto the night table, closing one button of her blouse to give her fidgeting fingers something to do.

"Why shouldn't I be scared? How do I know this isn't just the beginning? Maybe one of these days you'll walk in here and you'll be dead. Do I need that?"

"If it's Lilio," Eric reasoned. "He must be pretty scared himself."

"That's supposed to make me feel better, I suppose." She folded her legs under her on the bed and rested her elbows on her knees. "If he's scared enough to bother at all, he's not going to stop with half measures."

"But then again, maybe it isn't Lilio." The nicotine tasted unusually bitter. His tongue felt around and discovered a series of gashes in his lip.

"I'm not consoled." She saw him touching the split swellings and brought merthiolate from the bathroom and dabbed it over the wounds.

"Look, let's be reasonable," she continued. "I don't know about your friends, but I do know about mine. What we've got on the chubby one is not exactly tiddle-dee-winks. Of course

I've spared you the details, but how does he know that? From where he's sitting, you are a potential blackmailer. Extortionist extraordinary."

"And yourself?"

"Yes. Me too."

"Then how about you clearing out, for a starter?"

His challenge whizzed right by her without examination. She smiled quietly to herself and flicked an ash on the floor. "Nothing ever happens to me," she said. "I lead a charmed life."

"Yeah. Like the hospital," he answered, wrinkling his forehead.

"Well, forget it," she moved closer to him, taking care not to jounce the bed. "I don't run from anybody. At least not alone. If you go, I'll go along. Just to sponge off you, of course."

"Then forget it," he said with decision. "Because I stay here."

"You must have pretty good reasons."

He met her statement with a grunt. Whether he had good reasons or not, he wasn't the rabbit who ran. Gingerly he got out of bed and went to look at himself. His face resembled a blue sack of potatoes, the left eye practically closed, his lower lip sticking out clownishly. "Gad. It's been a long time since I looked like this."

"Seems to me you're enjoying it."

No, he wasn't enjoying it. He held a bundle of fury tight inside him. Only this wasn't the time to unloose it. He needed brains now, not anger. He had to find out who was after him. You didn't get the answer by raging. Plenty of opportunity for that when he knew more.

"One thing puzzles me," Cee-Zee interrupted his thoughts. "Why you haven't sicked the cops on Lilio anyway."

He turned from the mirror, glad not to have to look at himself any longer. "The answer is simple. You weren't for that idea. When you clammed up about him, I decided to let you scamper around on your nice long rope."

"Is now the time?" she asked.

"Not unless you want to clue me in on all the paragraphs."

She shook her head.

"Okay, then. I don't do anything till you talk first."

He wasn't going to try to worm it out of her. That, too, would come in its own good time, he thought. Or at least, so he hoped.

Right now, though, he had to concentrate on getting himself back into shape. He couldn't go prowling around with a mug that looked like a hundred horses ran over it. And confined to the house, there wasn't much else he could do but play footsies with Cee-Zee. He scowled at the telephone, thinking it was his only source of supply and a pretty poor source at that. Sure, he could call Donald and feel him out. But Donald knew how to play with words.

Somehow he couldn't get Donald out of his mind. A sixth sense told him that Lilio wouldn't have waited this long for the strong arming job. But Donald, who didn't have the guts or the physical strength to fight back himself, was the more likely prospect. That was okay with him. If he could pry Donald loose from his confidence, then Robin could more easily see what her brother was made of. He hoped that it was Donald. He almost prayed for it.

"So here we are," Cee-Zee said, coming up behind him. "What do we do for entertainment?"

His mushy face distorted into a semblance of a grin. He flicked at the rosette on her bra. "I don't know. Got any suggestions?"

"We can have a party," she said, teasing him. "Invite all the big shots. The mayor. The governor. Whoever you like."

He touched his cheek. "I feel strangely anti-social."

The afternoon sun had begun to cool down, its burnished color fading from the room. Kids home from school yelled at each other across the traffic outside, lending a touch of intimacy to their own lowered voices.

"You're feeling sorry for yourself," she said. "And I don't blame you."

"Bull."

"Well, I really don't, poor thing. You're fun when you aren't losing your temper, Spooky. I really like you. Once in a while, anyway." She took one of his hands and placed it on the hollow of her throat.

He felt the silky dusting powder on her skin and smelled its subtle fragrance.

"I can be gentle," she said, "with an invalid." She took a step closer to him and lifted his hand now to her lips. "I can be sweet and soothing." She spoke with her eyes closed. "Wouldn't that be nice for a change? Like two babies playing in the play pen. You can teethe on my nipples."

"What a line," he groaned. But he didn't move away from her.

She took him over to the bed and made him sit down. Carefully avoiding his bruises, she snuggled closer, drawing small ovals on his chest with her tongue.

"We can play nice quiet games till you're all better," she said, without lifting her head away from him.

"Nice quiet games." He stroked the nape of her neck.

He counted back to the last time they'd gone to bed together. Quite a while for a girl so accustomed to popping in and out whenever the urge came. He felt the intensity lurking within her body.

"Take down my hair," she whispered.

He moved his fingers into the blonde mass and pulled out the few pins. Her hair tumbled warm and soft over him. He liked this hair, he liked everything physical about her.

"Take off my blouse."

He undid the single button and slid the thin cloth over her shoulders. He stroked them with his palm and felt the same powdered silkiness.

"My bra."

He pulled at the hooks, then moved his hand around to the front, feeling the weight of her breasts sag down into his palm.

A wineskin of flesh, hot, yet somehow cool, the nipple beginning to harden as he circled it with one finger. She was being very gentle, very considerate, and he enjoyed her care. A lovely spring afternoon with this woman, out of time, out of space. What more could he want but to lie like this on his back and have her work on him. Cee-Zee's consideration was almost worth his battered face. He took her other breast and pressed them both together, feeling them hump in deep cleavage.

Her legs were already naked and the loose skirt fell from her, revealing her transparent panties, her hips and buttocks milky white beneath the nylon.

"Take them down," she said.

He slid his hands in under the elastic and drew them over her thighs. She wiggled out of them so that he would not have to move. Then he brought his hands up into her armpits to feel the prickly sensation of where she had shaved. All of her felt tender, half damp, half dry, like a new born calf. She put one leg over his thighs and began to roll back and forth, still gently. Her breath touched his chest in long vaporous exhalations.

He let his hands wander as they pleased along the tightening belly, across the slick round thighs. He felt lazy today, wanting her to do it all, liking the way she pampered his body, nipping him in the waist, tonguing his own lean hips. The contrast of her soft curves with his lean angles pleased him.

"Let me be on top," she said. "I want to be on top."

"Sure, honey."

He felt her rolling her breasts on his legs and his languidness skidded away, replaced by a tensing of his groin. The aching in his face stopped and his jaws clamped together.

"I see you're still good," she said with a satisfied giggle.

He lifted her up so that their bodies met in all the right places. "Damned right," he said.

"But I must be gentle."

"Forget that crap."

"It's tickling me." She reached her hand between them. "I'm good at massages."

She knew what she was doing and he loved her for it. The sheet began to slide under his back in movement with their bodies.

He felt her thighs tighten, playing up his desire.

"You got a brain down there?" he said.

"Two heads are better than one."

They were making conversation that sounded casual on the surface. But their words were like feathers, tickling, urging, inciting their passion.

She rocked back away from him and extended her palm. "Can you reach it?" she said. "I bet you can't." Then she began to sing, "Inch worm, inch worm, measuring the marigold..."

"Cut it out," he said and grabbed her to him.

The sudden clash of their bodies dissolved her playfulness. Now she flung her hips downward, wiggling onto him, her face contorted with the bursting of desire. The bed creaked and bumped beneath them. Her voice rasped in animal grunts. He thrust himself up at her, hitting and hitting. She flung herself against him and they whacked against each other loudly. He put his finger into her mouth and felt her sucking it hard, not even realizing what she was doing.

"Not yet," she said around his finger as his other arm flexed in the small of her back. "Hold off for awhile. Just a... few..."

She did not need to finish the sentence. She almost bit through the skin of his finger as the rest of her contracted. In response he slammed himself upward, almost knocking her over his head against the wall. But she hung onto him as their bodies became two halves of the same being.

They lay at opposite ends of the soaked sheet. "You knocked me out," she sighed, a happy smile softening her features.

Eric raised himself on one elbow. "Any time, chickadee. You name it."

"I only wish we could stay this way." She was looking at his face now.

"I thought you thrived on trouble."

"Harmless trouble, yes," she said. "For all I know, you'll be a corpse tomorrow."

"Never." He laughed for her sake. But his mind clouded with the prospect of what the next step would be in this circle of complications tightening around him. The next gambit was his to make. And he'd better make it good.

CHAPTER TWELVE

For two days he growled around the house, waiting for his eye lids to open and his mouth to take on the semblance of normalcy. When he went out to get some aspirin, eggs and beer, women edged away from him carefully. He looked like a bum in good clothes who had strayed in off the Bowery.

And the telephone didn't let up. All the frustrated secretaries in the office called to find out if he had polio or was run over or what.

In the middle of all this confusion came the everlasting voice of Hilda. He could do nothing that would make her stop phoning. There was nothing she wouldn't do to keep her contact with him alive.

But his eyes burned bright on the vision of Donald. The more he thought about it, the more Cee-Zee wanted to know the source of his anger.

"How do you get a guy seduced who hates your guts?" he finally blurted.

"That depends," she offered, nibbling on a pretzel. "If you're the one who's doing the seducing, it could be pretty difficult. But if you're not in the picture, I don't see that there's much of a problem."

She had said this to him before, but it hadn't penetrated. Now he understood how Cee-Zee's mind was working. But he wasn't going to let her go after this guy on her own. Too unpredictable. Maybe dangerous.

"You keep your nose out of this," he said, pointing a finger at her.

"Well, you asked me for the favor, didn't you?"

"That was then."

"And the episode down in the hall changed things?"

"Definitely."

She laughed at him silently. No doubt she didn't believe that anybody except Lilio had been responsible. She could think what she wanted, so long as she didn't try to do anything rash on her own. But he had no immediate worries on that score. She couldn't find Donald even if she wanted to unless she connected him with the number she'd called. And she had no reason to do that.

"Just shut up and recuperate," he said to her.

"You too."

They lapsed into another day of silence.

The week was drawing to its inevitable close and he had done nothing, thought nothing of any value. Any day now, Robin would be back and he still looked like hell. That would make a fine impression on her.

In the meantime Cee-Zee, trapped along with him, began to clean up the house because she had nothing better to do. She did it without getting in his way, silently, cat-like. He only noticed after the job was complete and he wasn't sure he liked the idea.

"What did you go and do that for?" he said belligerently.

"Mind your own business."

He was looking for a fight but he held himself in check. The fight he wanted wasn't, after all, with Cee-Zee. "And look," he said, to get the anger out of his system, "if that other bitch calls here once more, tell her I'm married, tell her I'm dead, but get rid of her."

"I think you're going stir crazy," Cee-Zee commented mildly.

"You're right."

Face or no face, he couldn't stay cooped up another hour. "Why don't we go for a ride?" he said. "You haven't been out of the house for weeks."

"I'm not anxious."

"Oh?" He stopped for a moment to see just what was happening with her. He always took Cee-Zee for granted. Nothing scared her, nothing worried her. At least, so he'd thought. Now he inspected more closely.

"I've got my own reasons," she said, anticipating him.

He didn't have the patience to go into it. "Then I'm going by myself."

"Who's stopping you?"

On his way down the steps Eric passed a Western Union messenger coming up. He stood there in the middle of the flight, watching to see. His hunch was right. He saw the boy knock on his own door. He came back up the steps and took the yellow envelope out of Cee-Zee's hands. He had it torn half open before she stopped him.

"You're pretty nervous," she said. "That's for me."

He looked at the name in the glassine window. "Sorry," he said, handing it back to her.

"Expecting something?" she said.

"Maybe. Go on, open it."

"Later."

"You're expecting something too." He took it away from her and finished opening it. "Says here, 'Long time no see. Get in touch. LILIO.' " He looked at her, waiting.

"Now do you believe me?" she said, her voice shaking a little.

He couldn't tell whether it was from anger or fear. "Doesn't mean a thing. He wants to see you, that's all. Doesn't mean he sent his bozos after me."

She grabbed the telegram and crumpled it. "What do you know about the way he thinks?"

"All right, I don't know. And I care less. What are you going to do about the love note?"

"See him, of course."

"*Of course?* If you think I'm going to fish you out of there a second time, you're out of your mind, girl." He had her by the shoulders and his fingers dug into her flesh.

"I didn't ask you to come after me in the first place," she said, her voice very low.

Her words stumped him. His hands fell away from her. He picked up the crumpled telegram lying near the sole of his wing-tipped shoe and dropped it into the waste paper basket. "Are you looking to get killed or sent up or what? I don't figure you."

She walked away from him and got a lipstick out of her purse. She hadn't worn make-up since she got out of the hospital. As she put it on now, the color glared on her mouth. "So you don't figure me," she said, regarding herself in the mirror. "I can't help that."

"If you take one step in his direction, we're through. No friendship. No nothing. And you better hear this because I mean what I say."

"I hear you." She pulled her hair back from her temples and tied it with a fragment of turquoise ribbon. "So I'll take my box of oatmeal and go to California. If it rains, I'll have cereal for breakfast. If not, I'll eat the oats dry." She shook the metal lipstick at him. "Now you listen to this, big shot. There's a future for me someplace and it's not here in this two bit hole with a stuffy bag of potatoes who hasn't got the sense to keep himself from getting all mashed up. I like you fine but you're just another ego in pants crawling around the face of this earth who thinks he's ten feet tall. Yeah, you saved me. I don't know for what, but you saved me. That was good for yesterday. And today is today. So pull your fat tongue back into your head and resign yourself. Nobody —not you, not me—nobody ever gets anywhere worth going by sitting around and using his brains all day long. Brains aren't big enough. There's got to be a heart somewhere. And you haven't got what it takes." She dropped the lipstick on the dresser and began stroking a tiny brush over her eyelashes.

The weeks of frustration over Cee-Zee suddenly melted in one bright glow of success. He couldn't keep his face from grinning broadly so he turned around in order not to give himself away. Her speech of accusation was not that at all, whether she knew it or not. It was the prettiest speech of frustration and jealousy he had ever heard from a woman. In effect she had told him she couldn't walk all over him and this was the one thing Cee-Zee needed to do with a man so that she could remain safe in her swaddling of contempt. Yes, he had the secret of her all right and it was working out just fine.

But now the time had come for strong arm tactics. "I'm sorry, my dear, but you're not going. If I have to tie you to the bed for a year, you're not going to mess with Lilio again."

He turned to see what effect his words had on her.

Her face was rigid with cold fury. She pretended to ignore him, continuing with the application of make-up that was gradually transforming her features into a whore's mask. Her eyelashes fanned out black from too heavy an application of mascara. The pencilled underlids were hard and almond shaped. She stood now enlarging the beauty mark high on her cheek, twirling the brown pencil carefully.

"So don't give me any more trouble," he concluded in a low voice.

She dug into her purse and brought out the amethyst earrings and screwed them onto her lobes, her chin tilted rebelliously high. He sat down in the living room and waited to see how far she would try to oppose him. He heard her pull the wrapper off a piece of gum, roll it into a ball and drop it with a small plink onto the floor. She padded to the closet and worked her feet into the high heels. They clicked around the room as she donned the remainder of her clothing.

The full picture of her now hurt him. He knew this brashness was a pose. She didn't need to leave her blouse unbuttoned so far down to reveal the ample breasts. Nor did she need the half a dozen bracelets jangling on her wrist to call attention to herself.

She passed him without saying a word, on her way to the door.

He bounced up out of the chair and pulled her back. "I said you're not going." The words came out from between clenched teeth.

"You lousy bastard," she wrenched herself free. "You gonna sit at the door with a shotgun?"

"If necessary. But it won't be. One more word out of you and I'll mess your face up worse than mine so Lilio'll toss you out on your ass. And you should be grateful."

"All right, mess me up." She swung her purse at him. The leather strap stung against his swollen eye.

He pulled it out of her hand and flung it against the wall. Then he slapped her down till she crumpled to her knees on the floor.

"That's how it is," he said finally. "Better understand it now."

He wanted to help her up but she kicked at him as he bent over. How long it would take her to cool down, he didn't know. But better an angry girl, hating his guts, than a dead one. For all her talk and lousy sense, she wasn't someone he could dispense with so easily. A peculiar twist of affection controlled him. It could goad him into anything that would keep Cee-Zee from finishing herself off with Lilio. He couldn't look at her crawling away from him on the floor.

She pushed her shoes off and stood up far away from him. "All right," she said. "All right." But the threat was the weakened threat of a tamed panther.

They studied each other's beat up faces and this time Eric went to get her a cold cloth.

CHAPTER THIRTEEN

At dawn the next morning, Robin's telegram arrived, asking him to meet her at two that afternoon. The door bell had awakened Cee-Zee and she watched him from the bed. She did not question him. All of her had taken on a cat like attitude. The usual laughter in her eyes was two burning points. She waited silently, biding her time. Eric knew that he could not trust her to stay here. If he left her alone, she would take off for Lilio.

He folded the message and stuck it beneath the appointment pad. There must be some way of preventing Cee-Zee from running headlong into destruction.

But if he stayed with her, any further progress with Robin was out of the question. He had no way of getting in touch with Robin. And even if he could postpone their meeting, he could not guard Cee-Zee forever.

In the semi-light, he felt her enjoying his dilemma.

Impulsively he decided to try convincing her one last time. Yet everything he had to say was already said. He sat down beside her and spread his hands on his knees, staring at his blunt fingernails as though they might give up the secret of potent words.

"Don't even try," she said, anticipating him.

He had to smile in spite of himself. Her determination to overrule him seemed more important than anything in the world. She would give up a fortune, she would go to hell and back if only it would take him down far enough for her to step on him. He had seen this kind of short-sightedness before. A peculiarly feminine trait that left him helpless.

"There's nothing to try," he began slowly. "But I want to tell you the facts, all the facts. Then maybe you'll understand why I had to be rough with you."

Her life was more important to him than keeping Robin's secret. Gradually he told her what was happening. He explained why he couldn't have gone away with her yesterday. Detail by detail, he shared with her the responsibility he felt toward Robin and how she was threatened by her brother.

Cee-Zee listened without replying. He couldn't tell whether or not she agreed with him. Yet, because he believed in the truth of what he was saying, he spoke honestly, holding nothing back.

When he had finished, he didn't ask Cee-Zee for her promise not to run out. He could only leave it up to her to make the final decision.

They ate a silent breakfast together as the day began to clear into a gray dull morning. A haze of rain weighted the sky, drifting in vaporous clouds.

As the morning progressed, shocks of lightning sparked in bluish white rivulets. He turned on the radio in an effort to cheer Cee-Zee up. She refused to speak to him. He opened a can of beer and drank it, feeling isolated and invisible.

"If I had any alternative, I wouldn't go," he blurted after the third can. His voice echoed back to him in his head. He glared at her at she sat in the chair, stroking on nail polish deftly. She didn't even look up at him.

He had no choice but to dress and go after Robin.

At last he stood ready to leave. "One last time," he said. "Try to be good to yourself."

Echoing thunder rolled above him as he climbed into the Jag. There was no canvas top in the trunk compartment. He glanced at the sky, hoping to make it to the airport before the downpour. As he drove, he went over and over the things he'd told Cee-Zee, searching for a shred of reason to believe that he'd penetrated her obstinacy. A cold drop of rain hit his cheek. He glanced up at the blackening swirl of clouds, then pressed harder on the gas pedal. Another drop, half a dozen, splattered the windshield. He turned on the wipers and saw them smear water across the glass. His hair got wetter and his shirt sleeves began to stick to his arms. Faith in Cee-Zee. That's all he had was faith. She couldn't let him down. She couldn't let herself down. His mind leaped ahead to what he would do if he came home and found her gone.

The tires sung along the glistening asphalt. Gulls swooped up beside the highway in protest against the rain. The salt wind whipped across his face and he bent his head low, driving fast through the slanting rain. He hated all women and their stupid, narrow minds. He cursed himself for getting mixed up with them.

A lone Ford rattled away on the right hand lane, ladders sticking out from the open trunk. He passed it easily and kept pouring on horse power, feeling the tires gripping the road, still with enough traction. He licked splashes of water off his lips and saw the leather dashboard become splotches of dark red. The speedometer needle hovered at seventy five. He wondered about the flight ceiling and if visibility had delayed Robin's plane. All he wanted to do was put her somewhere safe and get back to Cee-Zee as soon as possible.

Inside the waiting room, he asked about the flight arrival. A sleek girl told him the plane would be delayed an hour. He paced and chain smoked, betting that if he called Cee-Zee she wouldn't answer, if only to annoy him further. Yet his hand closed around some change in his pocket and he slid into a booth, needing to take the chance.

He let it ring seventeen times before hanging up. She must be home. She had to be. To go out in this weather, even for the few minutes it took to catch a cab, would bedraggle her appearance. She wouldn't want to meet Lilio looking like a half drowned kitten. The thought didn't console him. Nothing stopped Cee-Zee when she made up her mind.

He went into the bar and poured a couple of double shots into his gullet, feeling it mix with the beer. There was no danger that he might get drunk. Anger kept him sober and alert. The Scotch made his anger flare higher, fanning it into spreading flames that ripped through the dry brush of his body. He swung off the stool and tried the phone again. Let Cee-Zee know he was on her tail. Then he pushed through the commotion of people departing and arriving to wait near the entrance so he could grab Robin and hustle her off.

He couldn't make plans about where to take her. She had a stubborn mind of her own. There was nothing to do but wait and discover her mood, hoping that the week in Cuba had made her acquiescent.

He heard her flight announced and a few minutes later scanned the arriving faces.

Her hair sparkled with drops of water. She came toward him and he wiped one off her eyelash.

"Hello, Eric."

The same greeting, the same Robin, from out of nowhere.

"Hello, little girl," he said and took the round travelling case from her.

He had forgotten the beating, but now he became conscious of his face as he saw her examining him, her eyebrows drawn together in concern.

"Bumped into a wall," he said, laughing it off. "Forgot to turn on the light."

She sighed nervously, but did not try to object to his explanation.

"How about a sandwich and something warm to drink?" he said, steering her out of the way of people greeting each other with hard embraces. Fragments of Spanish mixed with the English greetings.

"You could use some coffee yourself," she said, sniffing his breath. Her nose and cheeks were a suffused pink. She looked rested and healthy and ripened by the sun. Whomever she had stayed with had treated her well, he thought gratefully.

He took her into the dining room and they found an empty table in the corner. She slid onto the cream leather bench and rested back against it.

"Bumpy trip?" he said, covering his impatience to get back to Cee-Zee with a casual demeanor meant to put Robin at her ease.

"I didn't mind. I'm glad to be home."

Home, he thought, wondering whether she meant America or himself or the prospect of Donald.

They ordered sandwiches and coffee. He really wanted another drink. His foot touched her valise beside him and he pushed it out of the way.

"You see," she said, "we do always sit someplace."

"But this time we're not arguing," he finished.

"Not yet."

Her hair had grown in just a fraction and it fell onto her forehead in bright titian strands. The sun had bleached its top a shade lighter and her eyebrows almost strawberry blonde.

She belongs on a yacht in the Mediterranean, he thought, imagining her slim body in a scant white bathing suit.

"By the way," he said, "I still have your car." He shifted the hard chair back from the table. He needed to stretch his legs. The calves felt tight. The whiskey hadn't done a thing to relax him. The joints of his fingers felt too large. He had to stop himself from clenching his fists. He wanted to grab her and get the hell back to the apartment. The passing seconds clicked loudly in his ears.

"Yes, I know," she said.

"Hm?"

"I know you still have my car. Why are you so nervous, Eric?"

"Just a natural reaction." He wanted to gloss over it. "How do you know about the car?"

"From looking at you."

"You mean the license plate is written on my forehead?"

She smiled kindly and played with her sandwich. Neither of them seemed very hungry.

"That's a poor joke," she said. "But something is written on your forehead, yes. I'm not so sure I should have gone to Cuba after all." She pulled the toothpick out of the bread and dropped it onto the china dish. Then she looked at him, waiting for him to say something.

"What are you thinking?" he urged.

"I'm waiting for you to tell me."

"For chrissake, *what* are you waiting for me to tell you?" He glanced around now for the waiter, deciding on another drink after all.

"About your face."

He studied her, searching for the idea behind her placid eyes. What she expected to hear from him, he didn't know, couldn't guess. He shrugged. "So I got mixed up in a brawl," he said. "What's so unusual?"

"Did you, Eric?"

"Did I what?"

"You're being difficult."

He couldn't tell her that he was preoccupied and that she was wasting his time. He felt tied to the chair, gagged and growing madder by the second. "Yes, I got mixed up in a brawl. Why do I have to repeat everything?" His voice rang a little too loudly.

She tasted her coffee and put out a hand to him for a cigarette. The palm was smooth, with just enough lines to indicate she had a destiny. "You know," she said, taking the match book out of his fingers, "this is the first time I don't believe you."

He heard the conviction in her voice. "All right. What do you believe?"

"You tell me. I want to hear it from you." She spoke firmly.

He knew he couldn't avoid her. "Are we going to argue again?" He could just as easily have told her the truth, but a niggling curiosity held him back. Apparently she wanted him to confirm her own thoughts.

"If I knew what you want to hear," he said, "I could make it up for your satisfaction."

She sighed with impatience. "All right, I'll tell you." She put her chin on the back of one hand, pausing to frame the words properly. "The way I see it is that you were going somewhere or coming from somewhere, it doesn't matter. You were alone and someone beat you up when you weren't looking."

"Just one," he smiled. "You don't give me much credit."

"Then two men, six men, what difference does it make? But you were jumped, weren't you, Eric? Tell me the truth."

Her face implied that he didn't have to confirm it. Perhaps his own expression confirmed the words as she spoke them.

"You took a crystal ball with you to Cuba," he said lightly. "That's not fair. What else did you see in it?"

"It's very kind of you to try to keep this from me. But it has happened before, Eric. All of this has happened before. I've told you that already."

"But perhaps you're seeing it differently this time."

Robin bent her head down. She ran a fingernail over the white cloth, then rubbed out the line. "I never cared for my brother's methods."

"You ignored them," he said firmly.

"I believed in him."

"Blindly."

"Yes, blindly." She looked up now. A gloss of tears made her eyes the color of pine. She swallowed hard to regain her steadiness.

"And now?"

"I suppose I have no choice. He can't go on scraping people off the face of the earth. Why doesn't he trust me, Eric? I promised him. He should know I wouldn't go back on my word."

"Of course you wouldn't." The waiter whom he had beckoned before came over now but Eric waved him impatiently away. He suddenly didn't feel like drinking anymore. He felt too close to success with Robin. "But perhaps there is more than trust involved." He hesitated to continue. To spell out for Robin what he thought about her brother might strain her credulity too far.

"You might as well say it." She gripped her water glass. "Whatever's on your mind, say it to me out loud."

"I think you ought to stay away from Donald," he said bluntly.

"Yes, I will," she replied, mistaking his meaning. "Until I have my thoughts in order. It shocked me to see your face. I can imagine what it looked like right after. I will stay away from him, since he doesn't think he can trust me." A tone of bitterness made her voice heavy. "You can help me find a place now, Eric. Away from the city. I don't think I could stand being even that close to him."

Eric finished his coffee. Both of their sandwiches remained untouched, but he ignored that. He felt one step up the ladder of accomplishment.

Before he paid the check, he tried phoning Cee-Zee again. Stuck with Robin now, he might be gone for quite a few hours. Less than a week ago, that was what he had wanted. Now the timing was all wrong. He felt like a dog chasing its own tail. He put the receiver back, unable to listen to the hollow ringing in his ear. From wherever she was, he could feel Cee-Zee laughing at him. The best he could do was hope that she was laughing at him from a safe place.

The rain had become a thin, steady drizzle. They couldn't ride in the Jaguar comfortably.

"We can use a taxi," Robin said, standing beside him and looking out into the weather.

"All over Long Island?" he said.

"You forget I'm a Millardson," she smiled. "It has certain advantages."

They got into a cab and he directed the driver to Hempstead, thinking it might be easier to get something in a college town, if only temporarily.

Robin was not fussy. Too filled with her own misery about Donald, she hardly noticed the rooms Eric rented for her.

The furnished apartment had a certain cozy feeling that he wished she could appreciate. The dripping trees bent their branches over one window and the country odor of rain-soaked earth came in through the half screen. She dropped her purse on a chintz covered chair and he sat her valise beside the maple lamp. Newly scrubbed linoleum carried the sound of his footsteps when he brought up the rest of her luggage. A band of the mirror was rubbed off from long years of service, but the solid dresser gleamed beneath the lace doily and gave off the faint smell of oil.

"Now what?" she said, standing in the middle of the room.

He had planned this to be a time of really getting better acquainted. But he couldn't think of that now. He couldn't think of anything except Cee-Zee.

"Why don't you rest for awhile?" he said lamely. "The rain will have stopped by then. Take a shower, maybe a nap." He added as an extra inducement, "I'll bring back your car."

"I know I was taking up your time," she said, opening up the travelling case and removing a small tortoise shell comb. "I'm sorry I couldn't give you a day's notice."

"So am I," he said honestly.

She didn't try to detain him except to jot down the phone number and slip the piece of paper into his pants pocket.

CHAPTER FOURTEEN

The cab took him back to the airport, where he picked up Robin's Jag and sped back to the city. There were a lot of things he had to straighten out with her. About Donald, about what she intended to do with herself. He'd bitten off a larger hunk than he had realized. He knew he'd have to speak with Millardson and clear the air with him too. But right now, none of that mattered.

He drove through the thinning drizzle with the hunch that he was hurtling straight into the center of mayhem. The hope which had carried him this far shredded away. Cee-Zee wasn't there. He could feel the apartment looming empty and quiet, surrounded by the brick jungle of New York. Nothing could be fiercer than the beasts in that jungle. Tailored, wealthy beasts more venomous than real cobras in real jungles. His skin felt clammy with fear for Cee-Zee.

He left the car sticking half way out of a parking spot too small for it and ran up the steps three at a time. He flung the door open and called her name, hearing his own voice answer. Only his own voice. A fever burned beneath the iciness of his skin as he went into the bedroom and into the bathroom still hoping to find her, yet knowing he would not.

The rumpled bed had been straightened. He flung a book onto it in sheer frustration, watching it bounce on the tightly pulled spread.

Then he dashed out again and drove across to the West Side, knowing Lilio's place was closed, but needing to see this for himself.

He banged at the locked door. An old woman from the building beside it came out and yelled at him to go away. At the corner drug store, he phoned everyone he knew to discover if by some slim chance, one of his acquaintances knew Lilio.

Then he stood on the street corner, his arms still, his jaw grinding, his eyes seeing red. And he decided to go to the cops.

But on his way to the precinct, he stopped again and phoned Martin Millardson. Surely he would know. Or the criminal lawyer who had smoothed things for Cee-Zee could find out.

Millardson said, "Come up to my office."

Eric had no time for formalities now.

"I won't give that kind of information over the phone," Millardson insisted.

He had to consent.

Millardson's plush offices in a Fifty Seventh Street skyscraper had just been redone in the most expensive modern taste. Eric tracked his dirty shoes over the new tan carpet and hovered over the secretary till she switched off the intercom and told him he could go inside.

He burst through the door to find Millardson swivelling around in his chair.

Eric put his fists on the broad desk. "I don't have time, Martin. If you know where this mug is or where I can find him, tell me quick."

Millardson eyed him and stuck out his lower lip in contradiction. "You have plenty of time," he said and turned his black shell chair around to look at the windows across the street, the rain drying on them in the first glimmerings of sunlight.

"If you're stalling me for a reason, let's have it. You know what happened to that girl once. I don't want it again."

"*Your* girl, Eric?" His words took their time.

"That's beside the point."

Millardson put his feet up on the windowsill and examined the tip of one polished shoe. "I don't think it is." He swung around now and leaned his forearms on the dustless blotter. "In fact, it's very much to the point, old man."

Eric stared at him bewildered, his temper leaping to high waves inside him.

The radio on Millardson's desk buzzed. He flicked the switch. "Not now, Jeanine, I'm in conference." He shut it off. "Well, then, Eric, shall we have a little chat? That's how my wife used to put it, a little chat."

He had never heard Millardson speak about his wife. His anger paused to gather a crest of curiosity. Reluctantly he pulled up a chair and sat down.

"That's better, Eric. Much better." He pulled open the bottom drawer of his desk. "Scotch, isn't it?"

Something told Eric that he'd better tread gently, that he was walking through a mined field. "Yes, Scotch," he said in a restrained voice.

He pulled out the cork and filled two squat glasses. "Took you a long time to get here," he said. "I expected you last week."

"What for?"

"About Donald, of course."

He couldn't make the connection between Donald and Cee-Zee. He waited for Millardson to clue him.

"You haven't even tasted your drink," Millardson said. "It's an excellent bottle. I keep it especially for go-getters. Like you, Eric," his voice faded a little, "like you."

Eric put the glass down on the desk untouched.

"I apologize for trying your patience."

"Well then?"

Millardson's shrewd eyes examined him, charged from appreciation. "I took the liberty of keeping an eye on you, my boy. After our agreement about Donald."

"You mean putting an eye on me," Eric interrupted. "A private eye."

"Yes. Donald isn't any Tom, Dick or Harry, is he?"

"You can say that again."

Millardson's shrewed eyes examined him, charged from the high voltage battery of his brain. "I discover, though not to my astonishment, that you are quite a man with the ladies."

Eric snorted and picked up the glass now. He couldn't really blame Millardson for checking on him. "So?"

"And what I discover is that you have not one," he held up a groomed forefinger, "not two," he lifted the next finger, "but three, pyramided into a very pretty triangle."

"So you think I'm messing with your daughter, is that it?"

"I haven't accused you. Yet." He put his hand on the desk top with a little slap.

"Believe me ..."

"I have not built my fortune on belief, Eric. But on action. I judge men by what they do. I don't give a damn what they say." He finished the whiskey and refilled his glass. "Now. My daughter is in Cuba. Safe for the moment, I trust. When she returns, I would like to feel confident that you will scratch her off your list. She may be a very little fish to you, no doubt. But to me she is the only one in the ocean. I have plans for that girl. And they do not include her coming to tell me one day that she is pregnant and has to marry some slick talker."

"I would laugh in your face if you weren't so pathetic," Eric said.

"That doesn't sway me."

An inkling of something deeper in Millardson touched him. He couldn't quite get hold of it to analyze because the pressure of Cee-Zee forced out everything else.

"You're wasting my time, Martin." With Robin out on the island, Eric knew he held a flush over Millardson's ace high straight.

"I'm buying your time," Millardson corrected. "Your girl for mine."

Eric stood up and leaned across the desk. "All right. Let's get with it."

Millardson picked up the receiver and got Lilio's address from one of his connections. "Remember," Millardson shook a warning finger. "Leave my daughter alone."

Eric hardly heard him. On impulse, he pulled open the center drawer of Millardson's desk. He grabbed the revolver he knew would be inside and disappeared from the office and down to the car, feeling he was racing against time. He could only remember the last time Cee-Zee had gone to Lilio. His blood pulsed hard at the memory.

The dependable Jag took him northward out of the city, heading toward Scarsdale. He knew what to expect. A quiet house in the most respectable part of town. A boody trap surrounded by a picket fence. The revolver felt lovely in his pocket. Heavy, solid.

Winding roads led him through a canopy of chirping bird sounds and the lush fragrance of hyacinths. Color heavy gardens nodded beside the road. He thought of Lilio infecting all this peace with his stink and contamination. He saw him doing his civic duty. The responsible citizen of a growing community. He thought of graft and henchmen muscling Lilio's way into respectability. Graft ... violence ... blood ... death. He thought of Cee-Zee and drove faster.

He parked down the road in the shade of maple trees. A leaf floated to land on the hood of the car. He got out and put his hand into his pocket. His fingers closed over the smooth cold metal.

Moving toward the house, he let his eyes fill with the spectacle. A long white stucco building with a terra cotta roof, sloping in graceful Spanish style. A trim lawn spread around it like green velvet. The wide porch was deserted.

He walked directly up the cobbled lane. His shoes echoed his stride. Scalloped window shades shut away any view of the inside but he could tell there wasn't a light on. The sweet vapor of dew clung to the shrubs and twilight drew fading streaks of color above the distant hills. His alerted senses absorbed the whole picture though his mind trained steadily on what would meet him inside Lilio's house.

First he tried the doorknob. The latch remained firm. Then he lifted the gleaming brass knocker and let it drop. Tensely he waited, knowing it was foolish to announce his arrival this way. But he couldn't get in through any of the windows without crashing the glass. He half hoped that Lilio himself might answer the door. Then he could smear him like a fat caterpillar on his homey walls.

The seconds passed before he heard a shuffling footstep. He did not recognize it. Not Lilio's.

A female voice asked, "Who is it?" Not a glamorous voice.

"Eric Spokane," he said with authority, thinking the woman might open the door to him out of curiosity.

His guess was right.

The door came ajar. A tiny woman of middle age looked up at him. Her pale features smiled uncertainly at the stranger.

"How do you do," he said, not wanting to make a commotion with the maid and tip Lilio off if he were inside.

"How do you do," her voice lilted upward in tentative friendliness. She opened the door half an inch further.

She might have been beautiful many years ago. But she wore no make-up to hide her failing youth.

"May I come in?" He smiled innocently, congenially.

She hesitated. "My husband is expecting you?"

"Husband? Yes. He is expecting me." He stepped around her and inside.

Should he believe her? Would Lilio keep a wife around while he played with Cee-Zee. The bastard could do anything. He looked at the pale eyebrows and the gnarling fingers spreading timidly across the skirt of her print dress. For an instant he felt pity. Then his heart shut coldly.

"Where is he? Where is your husband?"

She began to point behind her.

He brushed past her shoulder and headed through the parlor.

Lilio came out from behind the door, blocking him. They glared at each other in one instant of abrupt silence.

"Ah, monsieur," Lilio said, the two words like double fangs. "You wish something?"

His wife had backed away but she stood in a corner watching.

"Where is she?" Eric said. His hand remained in his pocket.

"Who?"

"Cee-Zee." Eric glanced around to make sure no one else was going to jump out from behind a door. "Come on, where is she?" He had no time for stalling.

"You are mistaken. I am all alone here with my wife."

"Yes," the woman spoke up. "There is no one here. No one."

"I said, where is she?" He grabbed Lilio's collar with his free hand. "You better talk."

He began shaking Lilio. The man's blubber shook and quivered but his eyes remained steady, two beams of piercing hate. He reached up with a slick motion and cut Eric's hand free.

The woman ran up now and tugged Eric's sleeve. "Believe him. There is no one here. No one."

Eric shoved her away.

"She's got to be here. Or in hell. What did you do with her?" He slapped Lilio on both cheeks. He kept slapping him.

The woman began to whimper.

"For the last time," Eric said, choking on the words. "What did you do with her, you filthy, rotten …"

The woman's little fists began pounding on his back. He pushed her away.

All of Lilio puffed up. His oily cheeks began to redden as he lunged awkwardly for Eric.

Eric's hand whisked out with the revolver. He brought its butt across Lilio's triple chins. The fat seared open. Blood rose in tiny beads and dribbled over.

Shrieks rang high from the woman. She started to run for the door. Eric whirled and dragged her back.

Lilio took the instant to grab a book end. Eric saw it arching toward him. He ducked and brought the gun up square against Lilio's chin. He staggered back and crashed into a floor lamp.

Eric dashed after him and flung his weight against the tub of fat. They landed beside a coffee table. Lilio grabbed one leg of the table and tilted it into Eric's face. The table careened off his shoulder. He swung the pistol, again tearing a ditch into the flesh of Lilio's cheek. Blood gushed and smeared.

"Tell me . . ." Eric's voice came full throttle. He crisscrossed paths in Lilio's face, opening his forehead, his nose, his lips.

The woman's shrieks echoed long and terrible.

"Tell me, tell me." He couldn't stop himself. The pointed metal exposed jagged tooths of bone.

Lilio blubbered and spat, drowning in his own blood. His heels kicked the carpet. He tried to fling Eric off his belly.

Eric jammed his knees into Lilio's stomach. His rage blurred everything except the desire to annihilate. Lilio's blood smeared his hands and soaked into his shirt cuffs.

The woman had collapsed into a corner of the room. She stared, numb with terror.

Lilio opened his mouth, spitting out mashed teeth with the blood. His hands swung wildly, blindly trying to grasp Eric. One hand found something on the floor.

A burning sensation ran across the back of Eric's neck. He felt his shirt begin to soak up liquid. He got Lilio's wrist and brought it around to see a piece of shattered glass stained with his own blood. He brought the hand flat to the carpet and hit the knuckles with the revolver butt till the fingers relaxed brokenly.

The gushing from his neck seeped around, staining along the front of his shirt. Ignoring it, he lifted Lilio's head and began banging it on the floor.

The struggle went out of Lilio. He lay limp. Unconscious, half drowned in the viscous red fluid. Eric sat breathing hard. He reached around and felt the warm spurt of blood course over his fingers. He was beginning to feel dizzy.

He staggered up and wavered over to the woman. She stared up at him, livid with fear.

Panting, he stared back at her, his vision not quite focusing. He ripped off a sleeve of his shirt and put it against the back of his neck, trying to press hard enough to stop the flow of blood.

"What do *you* know?" he said without much hope. "You know anything? I don't suppose you know a damn."

She shook her head in a trembling motion. "You have killed him . . ."

Her words had no meaning for Eric. He leaned over to try to stand her up. She cringed backward, pressing herself hard against the wall. He caught sight of the clotted blood on his fingers and the hand dropped to his side.

"Maybe you heard of a girl," he persisted. A drunken feeling seeped through him. He kept pressing on the rag. It felt soggy. "A girl . . . her name is Cee-Zee. You know her?"

She continued to shake her head.

"No. You don' know nothin'." He swayed away from her, dimly aware that he had to stop the blood or he would pass out.

Lilio lay like a stuffed toy, demolished and forgotten. His fat belly moved slightly.

Eric staggered off to find the kitchen while the woman crawled to her husband. She put her face on his chest. She wept silently and rocked on her knees.

He found the kitchen and pulled half a dozen dish towels out of a drawer. He stuffed them into his shirt collar. Then he turned on the water and let it run over his hands. The bright blood had begun to darken around the edges of the smears on his shirt. He splattered cold water onto his face and dried himself with another towel.

Then he started opening closet doors until he found a jacket to put over himself. His brain spun but he couldn't think a thing. He had to concentrate on keeping his balance and fighting against the weakness threatening to collapse his legs.

He came back into the living room, where Lilio had begun to bubble in his own blood.

"I missed," Eric said to the woman. "He's not dead after all."

He dropped the gun into his pants pocket and went out, trimming his mind for the project of driving all the way back to New York.

There was no place he dared go now except home. The car weaved back and forth on the road. He tried to drive slowly, carefully. His hands barely hung onto the wheel. He breathed deeply and blinked, stubbornly trying to clear his vision.

The towels felt damp but he could tell that the blood had stopped gushing. The fresh air revived him a little. The cloud on his thinking began to drift away.

With all the fury spent, he could reason better. He felt satisfied that Cee-Zee hadn't gone to the Scarsdale house. If she had, Lilio's wife would have betrayed it. Of course Lilio wouldn't bring Cee-Zee into that picture. He'd been a fool to think so in the first place.

The more he thought about it, the more convinced he became of the possibility that Cee-Zee hadn't reached Lilio yet. But if that were the case, where would she be?

In her own apartment in Manhattan? That didn't jibe. Maybe he'd hidden her away somewhere, safe from him. Especially safe from cops. But Lilio wasn't the kind to take such a beating if he could avoid it.

Maybe she was dead already.

His stomach went sick at the thought.

She couldn't be dead.

Cee-Zee never dies.

He kept the car going more by will power than force of concentration. All avenues of finding her seemed shut off from him. For an instant, he thought of turning around and going back to Lilio again. But a dead Lilio didn't necessarily produce a live Cee-Zee.

He felt all played out. Once Cee-Zee had said to him that brains weren't big enough. He knew now what she meant. He needed a thunderbolt, a voice from the heavens to tell him where to find her.

But he knew he wasn't going to give up. If he spent the rest of his life spading up every inch of earth on this planet, he would find her.

Cee-Zee never dies.

The words spun round and round in his head. A refrain that kept him going like hammering pistons.

Traffic from Jersey and upstate New York converged on either side of him as he came into the city. The cloudy thick smell of exhaust fumes began to erase Scarsdale. The episode felt very unreal to him. But the clots of blood stiffening the skin of his neck were more than real. They were the beginning of hell.

CHAPTER FIFTEEN

He stood in the bathroom and peeled the towels away from his neck. Then he leaned over the sink and poured the bottle of merthiolate into the open wound. There was no bandage in the cabinet but he found a roll of tape. Then he got a clean pillow case and tore it into strips, plastering them to his neck with the adhesive. A vortex of silence surrounded him. The bell had rung at the end of round one. He would take a breather and begin again.

With a bottle of whiskey he sat down on the reading chair, not forcing himself to do anything except drink the stuff. He wondered what Cee-Zee would think if she knew all that had happened. Her wall of defense had begun to crumble when she'd made her speech. He felt convinced that she wasn't a no-man's land anymore. He had managed to touch her by not giving in to her whims.

This puny satisfaction was all he had of her now.

He continued to drink, feeling the alcohol burn new life into his body. He felt tired, dead tired, but not knocked out for the count.

The telephone began to ring. But he sat with the bottle. There was nothing he wanted to hear from anybody.

It didn't stop ringing. He turned himself away from the sound and lifted the bottle again to his lips. The persistent ringing made him think of Hilda. She could ring till the Resurrection.

After awhile he began to think that maybe it was Robin. He remembered Robin with a start. Poor Robin, stranded out in the sticks. He had promised to get in touch with her.

His responsibilities to the girl made him feel lethargic. She didn't seem important to him at all. Very distant, the recollection, as though he were looking at her through the wrong end of a telescope.

He got out of the chair and went slowly to the phone, in case it might be Robin. He had nothing else to do anyway. But even as his hand dropped to the receiver, he wished it would stop ringing.

"Yeah?" he said listlessly.

"G'damn jerk of a fool!"

The words made him grin with new life. It couldn't be, yet it was. The thunderbolt. Personally delivered.

"Cee-Zee, are you okay?" he shouted.

"I don't know. I don't know anything." Her voice was serious, intense. "Get over here quick. I need you."

He believed her. "Where are you?"

"Donald Millardson. Hurry. It's Hilda."

She hung up.

He dropped the receiver, his mind refusing to imagine what catastrophe awaited. His sizzling brain released a second wind into his muscles. His hand remembered the pistol. He shoved it into his pocket and zipped the Zelan jacket on over his naked chest.

There was nothing he could piece together that would make sense out of Cee-Zee's words. All he knew was that he had to keep going. Had to get there. Had to see Cee-Zee with his own eyes.

When he came into the Millardson apartment, he realized with a shock that it was all inevitable. Insane, but inevitable. The missing links began to fall into place without anyone explaining them.

Donald was lying on the pool table, naked in the darkness except for one slipper dangling from a skinny foot. His head moved groggily on the felt. Occasionally he hiccoughed. A giggle punctuated his drunken silence.

Both Cee-Zee and Hilda were naked too. Hilda balanced on the window sill, half of her hanging out of the open window, while Cee-Zee stood warily at the doorway.

"Don't you come near me," Hilda said in the savage low voice he had heard only once from her. He knew she was drunk, drunk beyond reason, drunk into the need for self-destruction.

Cee-Zee's hand reached out to restrain Eric. "She means it," she whispered.

She didn't have to tell him.

"The things I've done for you," Hilda said. "I deserve to be dead."

Donald giggled again and shrugged his shoulders, the prisoner of some weird, inebriated dream.

"What are you doing here?" Eric said, because he wanted to keep Hilda talking.

"Not one step closer," her voice was barely audible across the room. "You won't touch me ever again. I'd rather die than have you touch me." Her voice cracked with horror at herself.

"She's been standing like that for hours," Cee-Zee murmured. "I kept trying to coax her inside."

"I can hear you," Hilda said. "Go ahead. Tell him everything. See if he appreciates it. He never appreciated me. Never."

Eric knew the truth of her words.

"He didn't even try," Hilda moaned.

But she had tried. To the point where she would come here to seduce Donald for him, thinking to gain favor by helping Eric to make some money. He felt sorry for her with a wealth of sorrow that clogged in his throat. There was nothing that Hilda could do to win him. And she knew this at last.

"But I keep telling you," Cee-Zee implored. "There are so many men in this world."

She seemed almost pathetic herself, in the semi-dark, her body shivering with fear for Hilda.

"For a slut like you," Hilda's words seared with contempt.

"Maybe." There was no fight in Cee-Zee's words. Her hand reached and found Eric's fingers and touched them.

"She thought that seeing you would make me change my mind," Hilda said, teetering dangerously over the open window. She laughed hollowly.

He had to chance it. In a sudden dash across the room, he grabbed Hilda's legs. She struggled and kicked, trying to wrest herself free, straining out the window, moaning.

He braced his feet against the woodwork and hung on, feeling her wet skin slipping through his grasp. The cut in his neck knifed fierce pain through him. His strength felt child-like, inadequate to Hilda's tearing desire to free herself.

Instantly Cee-Zee was with him, fighting to get one of Hilda's hands. She caught a wrist. Between them, they fell with Hilda onto the floor. She continued to twist, arching her back, straining away. Cee-Zee fell on top of her, constraining Hilda in a desperate grip that squeezed their breasts together as though in the fight of ecstasy.

Donald turned over on the table with a thud.

Eric sighed and shut the window. He pulled the drapes closed and flicked on the light.

Beneath the bright chandelier, Hilda's eyes bulged wildly. She clawed at Cee-Zee's face. Eric knelt and yanked her arms above her head to the floor. Sweat trickled into the hollow of her arm pits.

"You did me some favor," he said. "Both of you."

Cee-Zee opened her mouth to explain, but changed her mind. "We'll talk about that later," she said. "What happens now?" Her words came in jerky syllables as she tried to keep Hilda flattened to the floor.

"We've got to get her presentable," Eric said. "Where's the old man? Where's the maid?"

"Donald was so eager, he gave her the rest of the week off. I don't know why you thought he'd be such a problem."

"Circumstantial evidence," Eric replied. "I figured without all the facts." He felt disgusted with himself for seeing only half of the picture concerning Donald.

"Don't let him fool you," Hilda panted. "He's a selfish, mean, lying..." She couldn't find words adequate to describe her feeling.

"You could be right," Eric said. "But what about Millardson? Millardson, Sr.?"

Cee-Zee's eyebrows went up in amazement. "Who ever thought about him?"

"You mean, he can walk in any time and find us all like this?" Eric groaned.

"What more have I to lose?" Hilda said. She had given up struggling and lay defeated.

"Both of you better get some clothes on. And quick."

"You gonna trust her?" Cee-Zee said.

"No. I'll hold her while you get her things."

Cee-Zee disappeared, then returned with a bundle of stockings and girdles mixed with dresses and panties. She dropped them on the floor beside Hilda. She extracted Hilda's bra. Eric braced her while Cee-Zee put it on and hooked it. Then she slid Hilda's silk panties over her spare hips and yanked on the girdle after them. With a weak movement, Hilda tried to push Cee-Zee away, but Eric hung onto her and she finally subsided.

Between them, they got her stockings up and fastened, the seams crooked. Then they slid the dress over her head and straightened it out on her body.

"You went to her instead of Lilio," Eric accused Cee-Zee.

"No. I came over," Hilda interrupted. "Needing you for a change. Always needing you."

"I was so damn mad at you for trying to lock me in," Cee-Zee said, "I told her everything. Just for spite."

This sounded like Cee-Zee. But Eric wasn't mad. He was so dizzy glad to find her alive, he didn't care about anything else.

The collar of his jacket was turned up and Cee-Zee was too occupied to notice the bandage on his neck. He felt grateful for that. He didn't want her to know what he had done with Lilio. None of her business. All the time he'd been going crazy to find her, she was here with Donald and Hilda.

"Well, I hope you're enjoying yourself," he said.

"Quiet or I'll spit," Cee-Zee replied.

They made Hilda tolerable. At least she was decently covered. Eric didn't dare let go of her.

Cee-Zee pulled her clothes on, hurriedly tucking her breasts into the cups of her bra.

"Stop staring, glutton," Cee-Zee said.

Hilda winced. "Why couldn't you want me instead?" Her voice sounded like a prayer.

"You take that guy too seriously," Cee-Zee answered with forced casualness. "He grabs anything he can get. A real good for nothing bum."

Eric listened to her, noting that she spoke with a perverse kind of satisfaction. He sighed to himself. Yes, she was indestructible.

"Hurry it up," he said, recalling their circumstances. "I'm surprised the old bird isn't in already."

"Maybe he doesn't come home," Cee-Zee suggested.

"Not on your life," Eric said with conviction. "He likes to keep an eye on the kiddies."

He began to muse about Martin Millardson, understanding him with a new clarity. For sure he would be home tonight. And every night.

"How about Junior, there?" Cee-Zee motioned toward Donald as she wiggled her toes into a shoe.

"No," Eric said flatly. "We leave him just as he is." He smiled up at Cee-Zee's questioning expression. "And now we wait for the master of the house."

"We do?"

"Absolutely." He felt very sure of himself. "You'll see how to tie up the loose strings of a very messy package."

While they waited for Millardson, Cee-Zee made coffee and tried to pump it into Hilda. She let them move her to a wing chair, becoming very submissive in a guarded way that Eric didn't trust. She ignored her crooked stockings and rumpled dress as though her body were so abhorrent to her that she couldn't admit it existed. Her eyes stared fixedly and her mouth hung limp. She seemed to be staring fascinated at the horror of what she had done with Donald, condemning herself beyond forgiveness.

Cee-Zee held the cup to Hilda's lips, but she made no movement to drink.

Eric watched them, still preoccupied with his illumination about Millardson.

"You said Donald was willing?" he repeated.

"And how," Cee-Zee laughed.

This didn't jibe with the pact Robin had told him about. He couldn't believe that Robin had lied to him. He knew damned well she hadn't. Something was still out of whack. And he had a hunch that Millardson could straighten it out.

So they waited.

He didn't expect it to be a tea party when Millardson came home. He transferred the gun to the more convenient pocket of his jacket.

Donald struggled to sit up, then fell back again.

"He's really gone," Cee-Zee said. "Mixed everything in the house. Gin, rum, Scotch. I'd hate to have his hangover."

They continued to wait.

Hilda pulled her knees up close to her chest, trying to make herself invisible in the large chair. She wouldn't speak to either of them. Eric had the uneasy feeling she would never be the same again. He hoped that when she finally sobered up, she would seek mental care.

At last they heard the door bell, then Millardson's key in the lock and his quick footsteps across the marble, coming toward them.

He reached the doorway and stood there like a tightly strung bow, bracing himself against the sight of Donald. All the years of executive command came to his aid.

"You have fulfilled our agreement," he said briskly to Eric. "I'll sign that agreement." He took a pen out of his pocket and unscrewed the cap.

"Not so quickly, Martin. We have a few things to settle yet." He kept his place beside Hilda, conscious that at any moment she could take advantage of this new distraction to do something rash.

"It looks settled to me," Millardson replied. His mouth was a firm line in the sagging face.

"You tried to con me. I want the truth out of you," Eric said.

"You get my signature. That's what you bargained for."

Cee-Zee remained on the other side of Hilda's chair. "He didn't bargain on lousing up a woman's life."

"That is none of my concern," Millardson said.

"Yes it is, if we're talking about Robin," Eric said.

"I don't know what you mean." He came further into the room. "But I'm losing my patience with you and your interfering nonsense."

"You tell me why Robin is driving herself nuts believing something about her brother that isn't true. And why you wanted me to believe the same thing. I told you, I don't like being conned."

"You don't have to like anything," Millardson said, the edge in his voice getting sharper.

Eric felt a tug at his pocket.

Two shots rang wildly. A picture shattered and fell as something ripped through Eric's bicep, paralyzing his arm.

Millardson lunged to tear the gun out of Hilda's hand. But her fingers were limp as her head fell back, a gushing hole oozing blood from between her eyebrows.

Eric and Cee-Zee bent over Hilda. Eric shook his head. "No use," he said and pulled Cee-Zee away.

She nodded, biting her lip. Then, gathering her strength, she tore off a piece of her slip and pressed it against the blood trickling from Eric's arm.

"Now then, you vice-ridden, interfering fool," Millardson spoke just the slightest out of breath, holding the gun pointed at Eric. "You have tried every possible way to upset my plans. I could kill you both and go Scot free."

"That would be just fine, wouldn't it, Martin? And send Donald to jail on a morals charge."

"Shut up."

"No. I won't shut up. I've got you all figured now. You wanted someone you could trust to inherit the business. And you're a lonely man, Martin. You need company. The company of someone who wouldn't make you feel that you were cheating on your dead wife. Robin fills the bill nicely, doesn't she? Intelligent, attractive and respectful of you. But you had no way of forcing her. You had to do it through someone else so you would look like the innocent by-stander. That's where Donald came in. Weak little Donald. He would do your bidding willingly for the protection of his own financial interests. So you cooked up this pact for him to make with Robin. And it worked very nicely. Until now. Until Robin got old enough to begin thinking for herself. And that's where I came in. To help you blackmail your own son on a morals charge, trusting that Robin would feel the burden of Donald's shame and stick by you from guilt and responsibility. But it wasn't my interference that loused you up, Martin. It was Robin's own sense of individuality which you can't squash as you did Donald's. Too bad, isn't it?"

"You're very calm, Eric Spokane. But all the forces are on my side. I shall do as I wish with you. Your shrewd analysis will avail you nothing."

"I'm sorry to disappoint you," Eric said. "But you can't lay a finger on me. Not if you want your daughter."

Millardson hesitated for an instant, taken off guard.

"You see, Robin is not in Cuba as you think. And I am the only one who knows where she is. In fact, she's waiting for me now. And if I don't show up, she'll know what to think. All your excuses won't sway her." Mixing a bluff in with the truth, Eric figured he could chance getting away with it.

"I don't believe you," Millardson said flatly.

"All right then," Eric said. "Let me use your phone. I'll prove it."

Millardson motioned him to the phone, which sat on its long extension on the coffee table.

Eric took out the slip of paper, dialled Robin's number, then burned the paper while he waited for an answer.

When he got Robin's voice, he motioned Millardson to the phone and let him listen.

"I just wanted to tell you I'm on my way over now," Eric said into the receiver.

He hung up.

"Are you satisfied?" he said to Millardson.

Millardson put down the gun.

"We're going to get her," Eric said. "The three of us. I want to stand there and hear you square with her."

"What about..." Cee-Zee said, motioning to Hilda's body.

"Martin can fix that up," Eric said bitterly. "He's got connections."

CHAPTER SIXTEEN

They got into Millardson's Rolls Royce.

"You can drive," Eric said, holding his arm.

"I wish we could drop you off at a doctor first," Cee-Zee said.

"Plenty of time for that," Eric replied. There wasn't a square inch of him that didn't feel battered. But a potent exhilaration urged him on.

He had all the Millardsons in order now. And if he wanted it, there was a fortune to be collected because of the account. Something inside him flapped its wings in freedom. He could quit his job if he liked.

His mind went back to Hilda and the fate which had claimed her. He wondered if she wasn't better off, having solved her problems in the only way she knew.

Millardson steered the car along the Belt Parkway. He had nothing to say. The fierce shrewdness in his eyes had become the hazy dullness of defeat.

The heavy car glided silently at fifty. Only the ticking of the clock on the dashboard broke the silence.

"Brace up, old man," Eric said. "Maybe she'll forgive you. A little honesty goes a long way."

Millardson took a cigar out of his pocket and jammed it into his mouth, unlit.

Cee-Zee found matches in her purse and struck one for him. "Cheer up, little guy," she said.

Eric looked at her and smiled. He wondered what Cee-Zee was thinking behind her mask of control.

They came up the quiet streets of Hempstead and parked across from the frame house.

"In your condition," Cee-Zee said, "you're gonna scare the landlady." She smiled at Eric affectionately.

"You don't look so hot yourself," he replied.

She took a quick glance at herself in the rear view mirror. "I guess nobody ought to be sheltered forever," she said.

They climbed the steps of the wooden porch and Eric rang the bell.

The landlady looked at all three, her eyes widened at the sight of Eric. But he had already pushed past her and led the way up the worn carpet of the steps.

He knocked on Robin's door.

"Hello, Eric," she said and then caught sight of Cee-Zee and Millardson.

"Dad?" Her features broke into a large grin. She hugged her father and drew him into the room.

While she was embracing him, she saw the blood on Eric's sleeve. Her arms fell to her sides.

Cee-Zee said gently, "I'm Cee-Zee Walters, a friend of Eric's."

Robin waited now, her glance studying first her father, then Eric.

Millardson took a long breath. He rubbed out his cigar in a glass ash tray and watched the smoke die.

"Why don't you sit down, Robin?" Eric said tiredly.

"I don't want to sit down."

Millardson examined every object in the room, unable to look at his daughter directly.

"Go on, Martin, tell your daughter all about yourself." Eric spoke coldly. Better to get this over with like a surgical cut. He had faith that Robin's courage would heal the wound once she had the facts and had them straight.

But Cee-Zee sat down, trying to withdraw herself from the picture.

“I’d like to be alone with my daughter,” Millardson said.

“No,” Eric replied. He had to make sure that Millardson wouldn’t twist the situation.

“Well talk, somebody,” Robin said. She put her hands into the pockets of her flaring skirt. Her shoulders hunched unconsciously in an effort to ward off the unknown knowledge.

“Your father has something he wants to explain,” Eric said.

“Yes.” Millardson ran his fingers through his hair. He swallowed and watched the trees for a moment, rustling in the night air. “I have a few things to tell you about Donald. About myself.” He remained bluntly on his feet, but the rest of him seemed to be caving downward.

“Come on,” Cee-Zee said to Eric. “He’ll tell her everything. You can check later. Let’s you and I go for a walk.”

For a moment Eric wavered. But he couldn’t let himself trust Millardson.

He stood behind Cee-Zee and smoked cigarettes as Millardson told his daughter the details of what he had intended for Donald and for herself.

Eric watched Robin tremble at the words, then brace herself. The innocent forehead wrinkled as her father spoke. And when it straightened out again, the first trace of understanding remained in a line that would never be erased.

She did not speak immediately. She took one of her own cigarettes and lit it, while Millardson waited for some reply, some response, his eyes cloudy and helpless behind the thick glasses.

She didn’t answer for a long time. But when she did speak, something of the inner burden she had carried all these years had fallen away from her.

Sadder, but cut loose from a guilty shame, Robin was transformed now into a mature person. Eric watched her, knowing he had been justly rewarded for playing the interfering fool.

"It's all right, Eric," Robin said in a voice he could barely hear. "You can leave us alone now. Millardsons solve things their own special way. In privacy."

Eric wondered for an instant at Robin's power of forgiveness. But he saw the pride in her and the courage which he'd always believed in. How ever she worked things out with her father would be the just way, the right and proud way.

He came over and kissed her goodbye on the forehead.

Then he took Cee-Zee's arm and they left.

They stood on the corner looking at each other in the pale cone of light from a street lamp.

"We'd better get you patched together now," Cee-Zee said. And then with a hint of wickedness, "Maybe something was shot off."

"Not on your life."

But he felt tired and ready to sleep for a year. He let her get a taxi and they rode all the way to New York. He didn't care about the meter ticking away. No complications, no responsibilities touched him now.

They went to Eric's doctor. Eric came out of the operating room with his arm in a sling and his neck held stiffly by layers of bandage.

"You look great," Cee-Zee said and took him home.

He went into the bedroom and fell soundly asleep into a dreamless well of darkness.

For twenty four hours he slept.

When he awoke, he didn't know what day it was. Nor did he care. The bracing odor of coffee filled his nostrils.

"Hey!" he called.

"Yeah, hey," came the answering reply.

He turned over onto his belly and smiled into the pillow, dozing off again.

The next time when he came awake, he felt bright and clean. Automatically he wondered what day it was, what time. Then he remembered that it didn't make any difference. He was rich, if he wanted it. He was certainly independent.

"Anybody home?" he called.

Silence.

"Hey in there."

More silence.

Puzzled, he got out of bed and padded around, finding no Cee-Zee. He laughed to himself. Sure, jerk. What the hell would she hang around for? For a battered old dog?

But despite this, he felt good for everything. He went to his dresser and took out the camera and sat down with it on the bed. A voice inside told him he was never going back to the office. A loud, sure voice.

He opened the leather case and stroked the black Leica, almost expecting it to smile back at him.

Goodbye to women. Goodbye to trouble.

Though Cee-Zee had managed to slip away from him after all, he held her no malice. She had the right to her own crazy way of living, just as he had the right to his. Too bad Hilda couldn't have accepted this.

Poor Hilda. It didn't make sense to force someone into a compartment that didn't fit him. It hadn't worked for Hilda. It couldn't work with him for Cee-Zee.

He snapped the leather case closed and thought through all the magazine editors who would still remember him.

Then he hobbled to the kitchen and opened the refrigerator door. He stopped short, seeing all four shelves bare. Stark bare. Not even the bottle of pickled onions.

He felt his arm and tried to move his neck, cursing the fact that he would have to get dressed and go out for breakfast. Damned inconvenient.

But such is the life of a bachelor.

He found a pair of corduroy slacks and pulled them on awkwardly with one hand. The midday sun beamed on the toenails of his naked feet. He got some tennis socks and sat down on the bed to work his feet into them. Blasted nuisance. But he succeeded.

Then he found the blue canvas shoes that were his favorites. A long time since he'd worn them. He sat and looked with consternation at the untied shoe laces.

A key turned in the lock.

The sound of high heels became muted on the rattan carpet. He went to the door of the bedroom and saw Cee-Zee setting large brown bags beside the kitchen sink.

She sensed him watching her and looked up while she continued to extract cans of soup and eggs and cheese.

"You really awake this time?" she said. "It's been almost two days." She wore a lemon colored summer dress with no sleeves. The front of it buttoned between her ample breasts in mother of pearl. She wore enough lipstick to make her teeth very white.

He walked toward her, the laces slapping on the carpet.

"Do me a favor," he said and lifted one foot on to the chair.

"Isn't it aggravating?" she said, bending to the other shoe. "How indispensable women are? Doesn't it ruin the male ego?"

He snorted and turned away from her. He went into the bathroom and brushed his teeth and managed to comb his hair.

When he came back out, she was scrambling eggs in a new aluminum pan. The wide belt nipped her waist, emphasizing the fullness of her hips beneath.

He pulled a chair up to the table and sat down, remembering how she looked the day of her arrival. Remembering, too, how he felt. His nervousness hidden beneath a cloak of rebellion. For some reason, he felt very calm today. Secure and sure of himself.

"But don't let it bother you," she continued. "It nearly murdered me to have to phone you that day."

He knew she was alluding to the episode with Hilda.

"Doesn't it aggravate the female ego that men are..."

"Worthless, no good, fickle, rotten." She grinned. "It's very pleasant," she replied.

The eggs and bacon and coffee warmed and made all of him comfortable. The teeth had been filed off the edges of his nerves.

"What are you going to do now?" she asked over coffee.

"Mind my own business," he grinned. "Free lance. Have a ball. I don't know. What are you going to do?"

"Free lance. Have a ball." She smiled with innuendo.

He didn't feel that he had to beat her into submission anymore. He got up and went around to her chair and pulled her head back by the roots of her soft hair.

"You're a phoney," he said and pressed his mouth hard to hers.

She reached up and put a warm palm over each of his ears. Then she stood up along his body and moved in so close that their thighs touched. She slid her fingers around to the back of his neck, avoiding the bandage. Yet her touch was far from gentle. The snarling tiger of her body clawed out to him.

With his good hand he dragged her over to the couch and threw her down onto it.

The springs bounced her up, lifting her skirt above her knees. She undid the belt of her dress and dropped it. Then she pulled the dress over her head.

"Eager bitch, aren't you?" he said.

"Complaining?"

He sat down beside her, the damned arm a real nuisance now. "You used to be the hard to get kind. What happened?" He was laughing at her.

"Don't tease me," she said. "I'm too hungry."

She sat up on her knees and rubbed her breasts against him.

"I don't know if you deserve me," he played. "After all I've been through."

"Like lemon and lime," she said.

She crawled over to him and put her breasts against his face. "Don't I smell good?"

She did smell good. He put his tongue into the warm cleavage and drew it along the heavy curve of one breast, feeling the nipple graze across his eyelid. This was one bitch who really knew how to give him a rise.

She sat on his lap and let her head fall toward the carpet. He watched her breasts tumbling upward to her face, revealing the white skin of her diaphragm, somehow tender as though it had never been touched.

"Sit up, stupid," he said. "You'll crack your head in half."

She arced upward, the line of her ribs pulling gracefully. "Anything you say, boss man."

This was a new twist. "What do I hear?" he said.

She wet her lower lip for response and darted her tongue into his mouth.

He had to make one hand do for both. It travelled along her back and pinched her behind so that she jumped a little. Her nakedness pleased him with a delight that matched his feeling of freedom from the office job. She was an animal creature, proud of her body, grateful for the pleasures it could give.

She got off him and lay down on the carpet, spreading her legs and beckoning to him. "We'll be careful with that arm," she soothed. "Don't you worry."

Her eagerness was delicious. He got down beside her and let his mouth wander the length of her, roaming into the valley of her stomach and over her tensing thighs. Her hands directed his head. He heard her groaning with tantalized joy.

After a while she made him come up and hold her tight. "Do it to me," she cried. "Forever."

He managed more easily than he'd thought. The arm didn't get in the way at all.

"Hard," she grunted, "real hard."

She knew how to hold him and use him. They meshed like a superhuman machine, each part moving in precise rhythm with the other. Her eyes rolled wildly. She bit his chin.

He felt the muscles of her go into a spasm and he responded with a series of convulsions that sent sparks along his spine and up into his temples.

When they moved apart she staggered up and went to get him a towel.

Carefully she wiped all the sweat off his body, stroking his hips and his legs. He could see the bruises on the insides of her thighs and his mouth print on her breast. Her hair fell forward in perspired clumps over her face.

But though she had satisfied him, he couldn't relax with her. Not yet. Greedy for everything, something still hounded him. He had to know why she continued to protect Lilio. But he needed her to tell him of her own free will.

She had taken a sofa pillow and brought it to the floor for her naked behind. She moved closer to him and lifted his head onto her lap.

"Something's bothering you, Spooky." She stroked cool fingers through his hair.

"Nope," he denied.

"Are you thinking about Robin?" she coaxed. "I notice you haven't phoned. It's all right to call her, you know. Just to see how everything turned out."

He knew how everything turned out without calling. Robin would move out of the house and live her own life. He also knew that Cee-Zee was fanagling. She knew he didn't give a damn about Robin anymore.

"Maybe you want me to ask where you got that ugly cut on your neck," she said finally.

He felt like she was painting him into a corner. With Cee-Zee he always had to be careful. Always a challenge, never a bore, he could never relax more than halfway with her.

"I want you to be quiet and let me enjoy a few minutes of peace," he said, half meaning it. Ever since she'd come to his apartment, the routine of his settled life had scattered like so many bits of a picture puzzle.

"You don't want peace, Spooky. You can't stand peace. You're not made for the business man's routine. Early to bed and early to rise. If that were the case, you would have been happy with Hilda."

She'd hit home and they both knew it.

Eric eyed her suspiciously. "You name it then. What do I want?"

The sun warmed her breasts, showing pale veins in a network of pulsing life beneath the now placid flesh.

"I hate to say this, poor dear." She leaned over and kissed his forehead. "But we've got the same lousy poison fueling us. We're meant for trouble, you and I."

He wanted to disagree. He wanted to say go away and let me alone, I've got things to do. But an intuition made him keep silent.

"The only thing is," she continued, "when a person gets into trouble all by himself, it's no fun."

"Oh?"

"Mm hm. I guess I learned that. When I was all alone, there was nothing to pull me out of my own miseries. I sit here and ask myself what kind of a shnook must I have been to want to marry Lilio."

"Shnook is right." He turned slightly to look at her face. Her fine nostrils flared slightly as she breathed. "But what do you mean, *when* you were all alone?"

"Oh, I don't feel alone now." She laughed softly. "I stopped feeling alone when I picked up the telephone to call you. It was a big moment in my life. All of a sudden, there was you, you silly thing. And you could help me. Like no one had ever helped me before."

"At least you admit it," he said with satisfaction.

"I know when I'm cooked. And I know when other people are cooked, too."

"Yeah? Like who?"

"Like you."

She moved herself out from under him and lowered his head to the pillow. "Why don't you admit it too?" She put a hand on either cheek and kissed him on the tip of his nose.

He felt no desire to deny the truth of this. She was the one woman worth having. She wouldn't interfere with anything he wanted to do. She had no silly conventions or pruderies to inhibit him. Lemon and lime, just like she said. Neither of them was the shined shoes and newspaper type. She would go gladly wherever he wanted to go. Get into all kinds of scrapes so long as they were fun. Turn up her nose at nothing but narrowmindedness.

He sighed and grazed her chin gently with his knuckles. "Indestructible Cee-Zee," he breathed, glad of it.

"You want me, don't you, Spooky?"

He sat up and kissed her ear. "Maybe," he said, still thinking about Lilio.

"Maybe? What's maybe?" She got to her feet and put on his corduroys, rolling them up so she wouldn't trip. Then she got him a fresh cup of coffee and set it on the floor beside his knees. She went back to the kitchen.

He couldn't resist any longer. "I wish to hell you would tell me about Lilio," he called in to her as she stood beside the stove.

"Lilio?" She turned to look at him, grinning wickedly. "There's nothing to tell. I made believe I had a secret." She stuck her tongue out at him. "Just to aggravate you."

He reached beneath him with his good arm and threw the pillow at her head.

Then he burst out laughing, at himself, at her, at the world. "You bitch. You screwy little bitch. I'm gonna have to marry you."

She stepped over the pillow and came to put her arms tenderly around his neck. "And that, my gorgeous, scrappy hunk of beefcake," she nuzzled his neck tenderly, "was exactly the point."

He sighed and thought to himself, Checkmate, honey.

www.ingramcontent.com/pod-product-compliance
Lightning Source LLC
LaVergne TN
LVHW050956080826
845145LV00009B/2326

* 9 7 8 1 9 5 4 8 4 0 1 1 9 *